He Was Absolutely Devastating, Wearing Rich Black Silk That Made Him Look Like A Sultan.

Never in her life had Mariel lost her heart so thoroughly to a total stranger—or to anyone! But it would be insanity to think anything could come of it—she was a spy and he was…? She had better find a way to get her heart back.

The dark stranger slipped up silently behind her, not touching her, his hands gripping the railing on either side of her own. She felt his body warm the luscious silk she was wearing till it was a kiss on her skin, and pressed her lips together, praying for the strength to resist.

She knew nothing about him. The sooner she got away from him the better.

She would stay here tonight, but that didn't mean she was spending the night in his bed. And yet, if he made a real move, if he tried to make love to her—she knew she would find it impossible to resist.…

Dear Reader,

Welcome to the world of Silhouette Desire, where you can indulge yourself every month with romances that can only be described as passionate, powerful and provocative!

Silhouette's beloved author Annette Broadrick returns to Desire with a MAN OF THE MONTH who is *Hard To Forget*. Love rings true when former high school sweethearts reunite while both are on separate undercover missions to their hometown. Bestselling writer Cait London offers you *A Loving Man*, when a big-city businessman meets a country girl and learns the true meaning of love.

The Desire theme promotion THE BABY BANK, about sperm-bank client heroines who find love unexpectedly, returns with Amy J. Fetzer's *Having His Child*, part of her WIFE, INC. miniseries. The tantalizing Desire miniseries THE FORTUNES OF TEXAS: THE LOST HEIRS continues with *Baby of Fortune* by Shirley Rogers. In *Undercover Sultan*, the second book of Alexandra Sellers's SONS OF THE DESERT: THE SULTANS trilogy, a handsome prince is forced to go on the run with a sexy mystery woman—who may be the enemy. And Ashley Summers writes of a Texas tycoon who comes home to find a beautiful stranger living in his mansion in *Beauty in His Bedroom*.

This month see inside for details about our exciting new contest "Silhouette Makes You a Star." You'll feel like a star when you delve into all six fantasies created in Desire books this August!

Enjoy!

Joan Marlow Golan

Joan Marlow Golan
Senior Editor, Silhouette Desire

Please address questions and book requests to:
Silhouette Reader Service
U.S.: 3010 Walden Ave., P.O. Box 1325, Buffalo, NY 14269
Canadian: P.O. Box 609, Fort Erie, Ont. L2A 5X3

Undercover
Sultan
ALEXANDRA SELLERS

Silhouette

Desire

Published by Silhouette Books
America's Publisher of Contemporary Romance

SILHOUETTE BOOKS

ISBN 0-373-76385-9

UNDERCOVER SULTAN

Books by Alexandra Sellers

Silhouette Desire

*Sheikh's Ransom #1210
*The Solitary Sheikh #1217
*Beloved Sheikh #1221
Occupation: Casanova #1264
*Sheikh's Temptation #1274
*Sheikh's Honor #1294
*Sheikh's Woman #1341
*The Sultan's Heir #1379
*Undercover Sultan #1385

*Sons of the Desert

Silhouette Yours Truly

A Nice Girl Like You
Not Without a Wife!
Shotgun Wedding
Occupation: Millionaire

Silhouette Intimate Moments

The Real Man #73
The Male Chauvinist #110
The Old Flame #154
The Best of Friends #348
The Man Next Door #406
A Gentleman and a Scholar #539
The Vagabond #579
Dearest Enemy #635
Roughneck #689
Bride of the Sheikh #771
Wife on Demand #833

ALEXANDRA SELLERS

is the author of over twenty-five novels and a feline language text published in 1997 and still selling.

Born and raised in Canada, Alexandra first came to London as a drama student. Now she lives near Hampstead Heath with her husband, Nick. They share housekeeping with Monsieur, who jumped through the window one day and announced, as cats do, that he was moving in.

What she would miss most on a desert island is shared laughter.

Readers can write to Alexandra at P.O. Box 9449, London NW3 2WH, England.

to

Steve Aylott and Colin Moult
and to
Brian, Mark, Steve, Bob and Craig
who, during the writing of this trilogy,
redecorated the house around me.

*Ah, Love! Could thou and I with Fate conspire
To grasp this sorry Scheme of Things entire
Would not we shatter it to bits—and then
Remould it nearer to the Heart's Desire?*

—Edward FitzGerald
The Rubáiyát of Omar Khayyám

Prologue

———

"They have the Rose."

The line was silent as Ash absorbed it. "How?" he asked.

"They got there before me," Haroun said. "Two men. One said, 'We've come for the Rose.' She had no reason to challenge them. As she said, they looked the part."

"What does that mean?"

"Swarthy, apparently. He walked in and she said she led him to the coffee table, where Rosalind had told her it was. He glanced at the ornaments and picked it out without much hesitation. So he knew what he was after."

Ash muttered a curse. "Did you get a description? Apart from all-purpose Arab?"

"Not of him. His companion has a scar high on his

right cheekbone. Pulls the eyelid down a bit," Haroun said. "Now, does that sound familiar, Ash?"

"Half the veterans of the Kaljuk war have some kind of facial scar," Ash said. "Where does that get you?"

"Well, it reminds me of someone, and it'll come to me."

"Let me know when it does."

"What have your hackers found in Verdun's computers?"

Ash grunted. "What they've found is the best firewall in three continents. We can't get in."

Haroun paused, thinking it over. "Well, we've got to know how he learned about the Rose so fast. I'd better get over to Paris and see what a direct assault will achieve."

Ash hesitated. "There's an air traffic strike brewing in France."

"I'd take the train anyway. Faster."

"Your predilection for faster is just what worries me. You're too headstrong for this stuff, Harry. I don't want you trying to break in to Verdun's offices. A guy with that kind of firewall on his computers is going to have good protection on the physical plant, too. Go to work on one of his employees."

Harry was shaking his head before Ash was halfway through this speech, and maybe it was fortunate Ash couldn't see him. "That will take too long. We've got to risk something more direct."

Ash groaned. "We can't afford to risk something more direct. Michel Verdun is in it with Ghasib up to his neck. I don't want him cornered."

Harry said reasonably, "Ash, you've held me off from this for too long. We have to find out how much Verdun knows and how he is getting the information."

"Not to the point of risking your life."

"Why not? Your life is going to be at much greater risk in a couple of weeks," Haroun pointed out.

"All the more reason to keep you safe."

"Ash, we're agreed we need to get the Rose back. At the very least we have to prevent Verdun's agents from delivering it to Ghasib. We can't afford to trust anyone with this. I'm on the scene. Who better than me?"

Ash hesitated, marshalling his arguments, and Haroun rushed on, "Anyway, it's my fault we lost the Rose. If I'd been there an hour earlier it would be in my hands, not Verdun's. So I've got a slightly larger interest here. Sorry, but you can't stop me. It's a question of pride. You asked me to get the Rose, and that's what I'm going to do."

He hung up while Ash was still cursing.

One

The young woman, small but shapely, her lips a rich red, her wild red-gold mane held up at one side with a jewelled comb, earrings dangly, skirt micro-short, ran lightly up the steps and into the dim lighting of the hotel foyer. She was short and very slender, with a long waist and low, curvy hips. Her dark stiletto-heel suede boots were above the knee, her neatly muscled stomach bare between the hip-hugging leather skirt and the white bolero top, revealing a neat gold ring in her navel. A delicate butterfly tattoo quivered on her stomach. A smart leather backpack was slung over one shoulder.

The concierge smiled involuntarily as he watched her. Many of the girls who used his hotel were beautiful, mostly actresses and students supplementing their incomes. This one, who called herself Emma—of course not her real name, he understood that—was not the most beautiful among them, but she had a certain something. It always cheered up his Friday night to see her.

"Bonsoir, ma petite," he called. *"Ça va?"*

"Bonsoir, Henri," she returned with a smile, crossing to where he held up the key for her. She was the one he could not place. With the others he could usually make a guess at their daytime occupation, but Emma was an unknown.

She was unusual in other ways, too. Always the same room. Always the same client. Only Friday night. Every Friday night.

Emma was not a regular in the usual sense of the word, but on Friday nights she was here at eleven, whatever the weather. Henri always saved the same room for her for two hours, and on the rare Friday night that she did not turn up, she paid him the following week.

She had arranged it this way to protect her client, who arrived separately and came in by the service entrance. Henri had never seen him. Emma had not said so, but Henri could guess that the man was a known figure—a foreigner, of course, since what Frenchman would have worried about such an arrangement becoming public? The *président*'s own mistress and illegitimate daughter had attended his public funeral alongside his wife, as was only natural. But foreigners were odd about practical sexual matters, there was no denying.

Henri had found himself agreeing that of course the man could come in the back way, although it wasn't usual. Henri liked to vet the girls' customers, so that if there was any trouble he could be as helpful as possible with the police. He ran a decent place and kept in well with the *flics*. His pride was that he took no money from the girls. He charged their clients for the room. The arrangement between the girls and their clients was their own business. He was an *hôtelier,* not a *souteneur.*

But Emma paid for the room herself. Now she slipped the money onto the counter and took the key, smiling that smile, and he thought it a pity that she spoiled the line of her own luscious mouth by painting it larger. Her mouth was generous enough, and he had often thought of telling her so. But she wasn't like the other girls. She was warm, friendly, she never got above herself, but she was not confiding. He had never quite had the courage to give her the kind of avuncular advice he offered to some.

As usual, she ignored the elevator and went lightly up the wide marble stairs, and Henri watched with an absent smile till the flashing, slim brown thighs were out of sight.

Mariel put the key in the lock and slipped into the silence of room 302. A small night-light was burning. In the shadows the air of faded elegance that marked the hotel was a little softened; you could almost imagine yourself back in time. Before the war this had been a solid, respectable establishment. Then the Germans had used it as a military headquarters, and after the war it had never quite recovered its former status. It had been in steady decline ever since, but the furniture and hangings had been of good quality once, and although badly worn, still bore testament to the old respectability.

With the quickness of familiarity, Mariel locked the door behind her in the semi-darkness, leaving the key in the lock, and crossed to the window. She dragged back the curtains and slipped the bolt that secured the large sash window. When she pulled up the window, the night air blew in, the indefinable perfume that was

Paris. She heaved a breath, slipped her other arm through the strap of her small backpack, sat down on the windowsill and neatly swung her legs over the edge. Then she jumped.

She landed almost silently on her toes on the ancient, slightly wobbly iron fire escape a few inches down and stood while her eyes acclimatized to night. Overhead only the stars gave any light. Below, one or two windows illumined the small, narrow courtyard.

After a moment, keeping close to the wall, she started up the steps. The courtyard, if it could be called that, was completely surrounded by the brick walls of buildings that abutted each other. The hotel was four stories high. One flight up, the fire escape, last remnant of something that had once honeycombed the space, made a right turn and ran along the wall of the adjacent building for a dozen yards. Mariel kept close to the wall all the way. At the far end it stopped against the back wall of a third building, which sat parallel to the hotel on the next street over. Here there was another window, open just a chink at the bottom. Mariel slipped expert fingers into the chink, pushed the window open, leapt up, swung her legs through. Her feet reached for the toilet seat in the darkness.

A moment later she tiptoed past the row of porcelain sinks and slowly opened the door onto the corridor. Behind her head the word *Toilettes* was marked in chunky italic brass letters on the grey door. Mariel glanced to right and left as she stepped through, and although the turn of her head seemed casual, her gaze and her body were alert.

The dimly lighted hallway was empty. It probably dated from the same era, but the decor of this building was very different from that of the hotel she had just left. Here there had been extensive updating—sunken lighting in the lowered ceilings, the walls neatly painted in grey, grey carpeting on the floor, and brass plates or letters announcing the names of the various companies behind the doors that lined the corridor.

Mariel went lightly and quickly to a door leading to the stairs, down two flights, and out into another identical hallway. Only the names in brass were different.

Shrugging out of her backpack, she pulled out some keys as she strode down the hall towards a door with a brass plate reading Michel Verdun et Associés, and sent up a little prayer. She didn't start breathing again until she was inside in the darkness with the door closed, and the alarm code had worked.

She had been doing this every Friday night for weeks now. Sooner or later she was going to get caught. One day, she supposed, she might even walk in on Michel himself. She was sure he was often here at night.

If she did walk in on him, she had a story ready: she had been out for the evening, had lost her apartment keys and had come to the office because she kept a spare set in her desk.

Michel might be suspicious, but she hoped that he would be distracted by the signs that his employee led a double life, computer whiz kid by day, working girl by night. And that his confusion would buy her some time and the chance to get away. Afterwards, of course, she could not risk showing up for work again. Her usefulness as a spy would be over from that moment. But with luck Michel would never discover, among the many people he was cheating, exactly whom she had been spying for.

But tonight the office was dark. Mariel made her way aided by the light filtering in the long row of windows from the street, and the glow from half a dozen computer screens. At her own desk she tossed her bag down. First she opened the bottom drawer and pulled a few items out at random, setting them on the desk. This was set decoration. If Michel happened to come in, she hoped it would look as if she had been searching for her key.

Then she slipped into the chair and grabbed her computer mouse with one hand. The screen saver was a shot of moving clouds and sea, and was another thread in the fabricated character of Michel Verdun's wuss of an employee. Mariel's screen saver of choice would have been something closer to the wild starbursts on the desk next to hers—or perhaps a series of morphing faces. She liked colour and wackiness and excitement.

The serene sky dissolved, and her desktop appeared.

For a few moments Mariel typed and clicked until the window she wanted appeared. Then she grabbed up a pen and, on a bright pink Post-it note, copied the short list of letters and numbers that appeared. She carefully double-checked them, then deleted the file and exited. After a few moments the desktop would dissolve and her screen saver would reappear, leaving no evidence that she had touched the computer.

Mariel pulled a zip disk from a drawer, stood and, armed with the little pink square of paper, moved through the shadows and paused before an internal door.

Noting the first figure she had scribbled down, she keyed the code into the security keypad. She waited till she heard the click, then opened the door and slipped inside, closing it firmly behind her before reaching for the light switch. It was just possible someone in a building opposite might phone the police if they saw lights.

A few feet away, two bright squares of light showed

two identical images of a naked couple deriving a great deal of apparent mutual satisfaction from the close conjunction of their rather improbably endowed bodies. After a moment the fluorescent lights flickered and settled into a bright glow.

Against the wall were two computers on a long desk. Beside it were several tall black filing cabinets. These and a chair made up the entire contents of the room. These were Michel's top secret, dedicated computers. The room was off limits to everyone save Michel himself.

Mariel crossed to one of the computers. She dragged the wheeled chair over and sank down, dropping the pink note beside the keyboard, reaching for the mouse. The pornographic movie loop disappeared as the desktop came up on one screen, but on the other the couple moved tirelessly through their paces.

It was Michel's favourite screen saver. Mariel hardly saw it anymore. She knew Michel did it to annoy, and it was annoying if she thought about it. Under ordinary circumstances she would have taken a stand, but these were very far from ordinary circumstances. Michel was a man whose guard went down around women whom he was successfully sexually harassing, and it was no part of Mariel's plan to figure in his mind as a woman to reckon with. Mariel the Mouse was her role.

The real Mariel de Vouvray would have mentioned twice that she found his screen saver offensive and then would probably have kicked the screen out of the monitor the third time to make her point. The Mariel Michel knew lowered her eyes and bit her lip whenever he summoned her to some discussion while the screen saver was on. Which was something he did to all the women staff—too regularly for chance.

But that was okay. If she did her job right, she would have all the revenge she could want on Michel Verdun. And Mariel intended to do her job right.

Mariel was a corporate spy. She had ostensibly been working for Michel Verdun et Associés for four months—but in fact she was working for her American cousin, Hal Ward, of Ward Energy Systems in California.

Hal was the inventor of the world's most efficient fuel cell technology, but he hadn't stopped there. His work now involved research and development into a variety of energy alternatives to fossil fuel and the combustion engine.

And someone was carefully and consistently stealing the results of that research and passing it on to foreign-based companies and governments. The pipeline for the stolen material had finally been tracked last year. Michel Verdun et Associés was a *"détective privé"*—detective agency—based in Paris, with links all over the Middle East and, most importantly, with the country of Bagestan. It was Bagestan, and Bagestan's unpleasant dictator, Ghasib, who benefited most from the stolen industrial secrets.

Hal wanted the leak stopped. But Michel Verdun—as might be expected—had some of the best data protection software in the world on his computers. Hal had decided to put someone right inside Michel Verdun's organization, not only to discover the source of the leak in his own corporation, but to unravel Michel Verdun's entire operation, from leak to end user.

Mariel de Vouvray's father was French, and a not too distant cousin of Hal's father. Her mother was American, and the sister of Hal's mother. Mariel had spent every summer in California almost since she was born,

many of them on Hal's family estate. She was fluently
bilingual. She had taken her university degree in computer intelligence and then had gone to work full-time
for Hal. She was a natural for this job.

It had been a relatively simple matter to get her into
Michel's organization. Through one of his friends in
Silicon Valley, Hal had engineered the head hunting and
abrupt departure of one of Michel's key computer people. Mariel's fluent English and glowing references
from her mythical former job (courtesy of another good
friend of Hal's), added to her willingness to start immediately, had nailed her the post left vacant by the
departure.

Since then, slowly and carefully, because time was
not the most important factor, Mariel had wormed her
way into the most secret parts of Verdun's organization.
She had placed ''moles'' into his computer program-
ming so that her own computer was e-mailed a copy of
all his new passwords and codes every week. She had
reconnoitred the building and found the old disused fire
escape, and the hotel.

Every Friday night before she left the building at the
end of the day she went up to the fourth-floor toilets,
unlocked the window and opened it a crack. Then she
went home, changed into her disguise and returned as
Emma.

And then she checked the computers in this room for
data files that had arrived during the week and sent them
on to Hal Ward's own safe computer. Even if Michel
did discover that he was being spied on, he would not
find out where the information had gone.

Mot de passe? demanded the screen, and Mariel con-
sulted the little paper and keyed in that week's pass-
word. Then she summoned up the list of everything that

had arrived during the past week. Michel routinely deleted the files as he dealt with them, but Mariel had installed a mole on the computer that saved all files to a second, hidden folder. Since she had been inside his firewall when she did it, the program remained undetected.

Michel had a finger in lots of pies, most of which were rotten. He had agents, moles and hackers everywhere, stealing data and sending it to these two computers anonymously. He then sold it to his many clients.

One of the things for which she most despised him was the work he did for a Swiss bank. Michel investigated the lives of the people who were fighting to get back the money that had been deposited before the Second World War by relatives who had afterwards died in German concentration camps. The bank was hoping to blackmail vulnerable people into dropping their claims. He did the same for a multinational pharmaceutical giant, investigating the backgrounds of anyone—politicians included—who challenged them.

That was Michel Verdun. Very, very choosy about his clients—he wouldn't touch anyone who didn't have money.

Mariel scanned the list of received data with practised skill. Michel's system worked on a number code. Agents sent data signed with a code. In return he paid money into anonymous bank accounts. Anyone trying to sort out his little empire would have one hell of a time.

It hadn't taken Mariel long to learn that one code prefix always related to Ghasib. Suffixes sometimes were also apparently assigned, but she hadn't discovered yet whether a suffix related to a particular source or a particular job.

Of course Mariel's priority was anything with a Ghasib prefix. Tonight there were nearly a dozen. It had been a busy week for the Ghasib spies. And most carried the same suffix number.

In the past few weeks there had been a new suffix used on more and more incoming Ghasib data, but since most were encrypted she had not been able to glean much.

She opened each file before sending it, and read it if possible. Then she downloaded it onto a zip disk and deleted it from the secret folder. When she had checked and downloaded all the new files she would take the zip disk to her own computer and send the files off to Hal.

She never sent anything out from the secret computers. Michel's firewall was extremely efficient, and he had software monitoring all traffic from this machine.

Mariel lifted her head, listening for a moment. Nothing. Listening was an automatic response, making sure you didn't get too deep in what you were doing. She checked the clock—11:38—then clicked on the next Ghasib-prefixed e-mail. A few lines of encryption gibberish met her eyes, and she instantly exited again and clicked it to download to the zip disk. The next few were the same.

The last file had only just arrived, so Michel hadn't seen it yet. Mariel felt a curious presentiment as she clicked it open. Maybe it would be significant. Maybe this would be the break she needed.

Another encrypted message, with an attachment this time. Mariel bit her lip as she clicked on the attachment.

It was a photograph. The image slowly formed on the screen, and Mariel blinked and opened her eyes in dumb disbelief. It was no one she recognized, but it was the most gorgeous man she had ever clapped eyes on.

In her life.

Mariel sat gazing at the handsome masculine face while her brain circuits started misfiring, one by two by four, triggering off a chain of explosions that blew reason into the void. She knew about the reality of love at first sight. *Coup de foudre,* it was called in French. She believed it was possible.

But she had never heard before of anyone falling head over heels in love with a face in a photograph.

Two

Waving dark hair above a broad, wide forehead. Strong square eyebrows. Eyes dark with an intensity that seemed to burn her. A mouth tilted with devilment, passion in the beautifully shaped full lips, and a kind of wildness in the expression as a whole. Like looking into a storm.

Who was he? Mariel had a deep feeling of recognition, but was that real, or just the effect the face was having on her, as if she had known him in another lifetime, was destined to love him in this one?

She shook her head, trying to re-establish a sense of reality, and glanced at the computer clock again. She had lost her sense of time. Was it really only 11:48, or had the clock frozen along with her brain? She was suddenly frightened. How long had she sat here, staring at this not-quite-stranger's face?

It was her job to download the file, she reminded

herself, like a child who had forgotten the alphabet. But she could not bear to lose the face. Without any pause for rational thought, she dragged the cursor over *Print*. She clicked the mouse, heard the printer whirr into life, and then bit her lip with regret. This, she told herself, was the way spies crashed in flames—letting your guard down for one fatal second.

But it was too late now.

She downloaded the file to the disk, then deleted it from the secret folder. Michel would never know it had been opened.

Two minutes later she was still standing there, the zip disk in her hand, waiting as the printer ground back and forth over the page. The colour printer printed slowly, and it printed exceeding fine. What a fool she was! She ought to be getting out of here, but now she was rivetted, waiting. Printers were not her field. She was afraid of what might happen if she tried to abort the print. Would it spew the thing out the next time it was activated?

Usually when she had finished, Mariel locked this office before returning to her own desk to send the contents of her disk. But the printer was going to take forever. So to save time she went out to her computer and slipped the zip disk into the slot.

Michel had secret software on every computer in the place, which allowed him to recap every keystroke his employees typed. She was pretty sure Michel checked each of the firm's computers in rotation every week, reading e-mails and the history of everyone's cyber activity. If so, he never found any evidence of her Friday-night activities. Mariel simply disabled the program whenever she wanted an activity to go unrecorded. She did that now, then fired off the contents of the disk to

Hal's safe address, and deleted all record of the transaction before restoring the monitoring software.

She wiped the zip floppy, dropped it into a drawer, and went back to the private office. The printer had finally finished.

Mariel plucked the page from its tray, and again all thought left her head as her eyes fell on the image of that perfect, masculine face. What a devil-may-care smile, what eyes! Who was he?

So entranced was the spy that she did not hear the sounds of stealthy entry in the outer office. She heaved a sigh, flicked off the light, pulled open the door, and stepped through.

The man getting his bearings in the outer office was as surprised as she was. For a moment they were silent, gaping at each other.

"It's you!" Mariel whispered, amazed, as the world reeled and rocked and all the landmarks she knew sank without trace.

The man standing halfway across the office in the gloom, looking much more dangerous in the flesh, was the man whose picture she had just taken from the printer.

Haroun al Muntazir frowned and cursed himself for a fool. Ash was right, he was too impetuous. To break in to the office when someone was in it was the work of an ignorant amateur.

But the woman in front of him was a mystery. The brassy red wig and the black leather micromini and boots might have been enough to tell him what her profession was, even if she hadn't been so sexually alluring that he had the urge to negotiate terms with her there and then. But what was she doing in Michel Verdun's office?

When he managed to unfix his eyes from her, his gaze fell on the grotesque picture on the screen in the office behind her. A porn video. That went some way towards explaining her presence—did Verdun come to the office at night to indulge his extramarital passions?

Which meant he was behind her in the office? *Hell!* thought Haroun. *Just my luck I've broken in on orgy night.*

Then he belatedly heard what she'd said. *It's you.* What did that mean? Some kind of hooker's ploy to convince a client he was the stuff of her fantasies?

It followed that she didn't know her client by sight. Maybe she thought he was the one who had booked her time.

With typical boldness, he decided to bluff. He could get out of this yet.

"Yeah, it's me," he agreed. "Have you been given the details of what's expected?"

She nibbled at a corner of her mouth, unconsciously turning her red mouth into an exotic, inviting flower. Haroun's blood was too quick to respond.

Mariel quietly folded the paper she held, hiding the photo. How on earth had he got in? Her brain rushed to fill the gap—had Michel given him a key? Had the photo been sent to identify him to Michel prior to a meeting? Did that mean Michel would be arriving here?

Did his question mean this man was assuming *she* was the contact he was due to meet? She forgot the outfit she was wearing, what she must look like to him.

"No. Um...I'm filling in at the last minute," she stammered. "Michel—is sick. So if you don't mind briefing me..."

Haroun breathed a quiet sigh. The fates were being kind to him tonight. So Verdun's regular girl, Michelle, was ill, and the replacement needed briefing. Well, he certainly would enjoy briefing her, but the important thing was to get out of here before Verdun arrived.

"My car," he said, looking at his watch so that she would understand he was a man in a hurry.

She felt a surge of sharp regret that the face she had fallen for belonged to a man connected to a villain like Michel Verdun. Then her spy's practical brain took over. She wondered whether he bought secrets, or sold them. She might, with luck, pick up something interesting from him, and that would be the last of her usefulness to her cousin Hal. Because her work at Michel Verdun et Associés was finished as of tonight.

"All right, I—I'll just get my bag." She whirled to run lightly to her desk, as eager to get out of here as the stranger could want. She picked up the items she had tossed on her desk, dumped them back in the drawer.

It took only a second, time which Haroun passed in contemplation of the sloping hips, the firm bare thighs. "Let's go," she said, kicking the drawer shut. She had just picked up her bag when she noticed that the secret office door was hanging open. She ran lightly back across the room.

As she reached it, there was the sound of a key in the main door.

Mariel froze, her eyes flying to the stranger. In amazement she saw that he was running silently towards her. He was much bigger than she. He scooped her up in one arm and shoved her through the doorway into the secret office ahead of him. One hand clamping over her mouth, he pushed the door almost shut.

They were in darkness, the only light in the room the glow from the two horrible screen savers flickering on the computers.

His hand tightened over her mouth as the sound of the outer office door opening reached them. ''If you make a sound I will strangle you,'' the stranger whispered in her ear. Mariel shook her head, her eyes wide, speechlessly promising to be silent, and slowly his hand slipped down to her throat, where it rested in light warning.

A crack of illumination told her that whoever had entered the outer office had put the main light on. It had to be Michel.

Her only hope now was not to be discovered. And clearly Adonis here felt the same. But who was he, then? If he was afraid of Michel, Michel clearly hadn't given him a key. So how had he got in? And why?

He stood beside her, his body hard, watching through the tiny crack of the door. She could smell the musky scent of him, feel the firm muscles of his arm, his thigh, his chest, as he held her.

''The alarm's been coded,'' she heard a mutter from the outer office. Michel's voice. Who was he with? She turned in the stranger's hold and tried to see out the crack. One finger slipped up to her lips in warning.

Probably it was the danger that transmogrified that light brushing of his finger over her mouth into the most erotic thing she had ever experienced. Mariel's blood raced so that she felt faint. Her body seemed to melt with yearning for the hard curves of the stranger's body.

His voice rasped in her ear again. ''There is your client,'' he whispered.

Michel was just coming into her line of vision, moving towards the back corner of the outer office. He hadn't noticed that the secret office door was ajar, but he would.

"You can go out to him."

He probably planned to take off in her wake, but the last thing Mariel could do now was walk out and greet Michel. "No," she whispered desperately, just as another man came into view, his eyes dangerous and wary. "No."

"No?" The stranger's gaze narrowed, raking her face in the thread of light in a new assessment.

The second man had a gun. A small, square automatic. Mariel felt as if her eyes were glued to the neat silver barrel in his hand. Beside her, the dark man went still.

"Let them go past. Run for the door. I will follow," he whispered briefly, and waited only for her answering nod before pushing her to one side.

The armed man was just turning, Michel was facing in the other direction. It was now or never, and as the stranger whipped the door open and launched a kick at the gunman's elbow, Mariel tore out the doorway behind him and headed for the main entrance.

She heard the kick connect, a shout, and the sounds of struggle. Michel cried out in surprise. Mariel didn't waste a moment looking back. She wrenched open the door and dashed down the hall.

Behind her there were more shouts, and pounding footsteps. She hit the button summoning the elevators as she ran by, but carried straight on past, heading for the door to the stairwell she had entered by.

She burst through it, then turned to look out. The stranger was pounding down the hall after her, giving her a chance to appreciate his athletic perfection. She opened the door further.

"Ici!" she hissed, and a second later he came bursting through to the small concrete landing. She was already halfway up the steps. *"En haut!"* she whispered and, not waiting to see how he responded, turned and ran harder than she had ever run in her life.

He was behind and gaining on her. They were halfway up the next flight when they heard someone crash through the door below. They froze, and listened as the others went thundering down the steps to the lower floors.

Mariel breathed a prayer of gratitude, then crept up the last steps and through the door into the fourth-floor hallway. The stranger understood that she was running to a known goal, and wasted no time on questions. She led him to the door marked *Toilettes,* in and past the basins, and into the last cubicle in the row.

She was up on the windowsill while Haroun was still half wondering if she had led him into a trap after all. But with a flash of thighs she leapt through the window, and he was quick to follow.

"Close it," she hissed. "And go carefully, this thing is not very safe. Stay a few feet behind me and keep as close as you can to the wall, or it may come down."

He slid the window down and after giving her a head start followed her along the tottery fire escape, wondering if it would hold his weight. Ahead of him she turned and went down one flight, then paused. To his amazement, though nothing amazed him anymore, she hoisted herself up onto a windowsill.

He caught up with her. "Let us get down to the ground," he hissed.

"It doesn't lead anywhere—it's been destroyed lower down," she said, swinging her entrancingly naked legs

over the sill. He hesitated for a moment. Suppose he
had walked into an elaborate setup?

But now he could see that she had told him the
truth—the fire escape simply stopped two flights up
from the ground. No way to leap that without serious
damage.

She had disappeared through the window. Haroun
shrugged and, with a murmured *"La howlah wa la
quwwata illa billah,"* followed her into the unknown.

And found himself in a hotel bedroom lighted only
by a night-light. She was standing by the bed. A red
velour bedspread covered it. She was tossing two red
velour pillows onto the floor as he entered. He watched
as she tore the bedspread down to the foot of the bed,
dragged back the sheets.

Her black leather skirt was slit up both sides, and
revealed black lace covering a neatly rounded rump as
she bent and twisted, intent on her work.

He could appreciate such insouciant dedication to
business, and only regretted that he could not share it.
He wanted to get the hell out of here.

But he couldn't help smiling. He crossed towards the
outer door as she straightened. "I wish I could stay,"
he murmured, "but unfortunately…"

"Shhh!" she commanded. She now had the bed looking completely ruined, and pushed him out of her way
as she crossed to the window. She dragged it shut and
turned the little locking mechanism, then drew the curtains.

"Right," she said. "Now, look—Henri will think
you're my client."

"Henri?"

"Downstairs, on the desk," she supplied impatiently.
"Can you—" She looked at him, taking in his clothes

fully for the first time. "My God, you look like a cat burglar!" she exclaimed.

He was dressed entirely in snug-fitting black that outlined his body almost as closely as Lycra. Mariel blinked at the muscled chest, the powerful thighs, the firm biceps....

He cocked one eyebrow. "I am a cat burglar," he said dryly.

"I have to go down the front way, and there's no time to show you the service entrance. You'll just have to come out with me. Henri will think you are my client who doesn't want to be recognized, so he won't be surprised if you go straight out the door."

"And then what?"

"My car is in the next street. Can I drop you, or shall we go our separate ways?"

She was so cool! Haroun reached to touch her chin, and laughed with pure admiration. "I don't think I can leave you," he said. "Let us change our minds and at least make use of the bed before we part."

His words made her lips twitch into an involuntary smile. It was quite true that sex was in the air between them. How could it not be, when danger had chased so closely at their heels? For those who are truly alive, their bodies and spirits cried, a near escape from death is best celebrated through sex.

Mariel could almost have given in, too. He was so handsome, and when he was laughing he was pretty well irresistible. And she had fallen half in love just with his photo. But—

"You are ridiculous," she said sternly, though she knew he wasn't serious. "Anyway, we've been incredibly lucky so far and our luck would be sure to turn if we abused it like that."

He was eyeing her with a grin that melted her. "I certainly don't want the luck I've been having tonight to change. If we make love now, it will abandon me? You are sure of it? I think it could only improve. And perhaps it would even be wise to wait here until the search is given up."

"No, let's get out of here," Mariel said, ignoring most of the speech. "We can't be sure Michel doesn't know about that fire escape."

He was aware of a reluctance to leave her. He justified this with the conviction that she might be able to tell him something about Verdun that he didn't know.

"All right. We head for your car. Where is it, exactly? What make and colour?"

She told him in an undervoice as she opened the door and led him out into the hall. He went down the stairs lightly at her side, his lithe black shape melting in and out of the shadows. She could believe he was a cat burglar, but what had he wanted from Michel? Was it possible *he* was stealing secrets from Michel and selling them?

Henri was too savvy to take any formal notice of the sudden appearance of Emma's "client," and Mariel only threw him a smile and a twinkling wave before following the stranger out into the street.

Her car was two streets away, and there was plenty of pedestrian traffic under the neon signs. Mariel walked quickly, her high-heeled boots clicking on the pavement with little erotic snaps. She resisted the impulse to look over her shoulder to be sure the stranger was following, and instead tried to concentrate on looking like a woman on the job. She slipped her fingers into the little slash pockets of her micromini and let her hips swing in invitation. She kept wanting to laugh, and she couldn't tell whether it was the effect danger had on her, or the stranger.

At the corner she turned to cross the street and risked a glance back. Two women were offering their wares to him, jointly and severally, and they didn't seem to want to take no for an answer. Her smile died as a totally unfamiliar jealous rage swept through her.

She had whirled instinctively, ready to charge back towards the cosy little group, almost before she realized it. Then she took a deep, surprised breath. She had never been jealous before, and here she was, furiously proprietal about a man whose photograph she had first seen less than an hour ago! Was she going crazy?

Maybe it was just the effect of the danger. Danger heightened the emotions, she had always heard that. But still she stood glaring down the street as he smiled his regrets and passed the hungry hookers by. One of them glanced up and saw Mariel staring, saw that the man was following her, and started screaming at her in very pungent street French.

"Get off my beat, *putain!*"

"*Va-t'en, vache!*" Mariel called back, partly for the hell of it, and partly to stay in character in case anyone was watching.

Perhaps a little too much in character. The two hookers erupted with fury at her show of defiance and took after her. Fortunately the light had changed. Mariel ran across the busy street, followed by the cat burglar, who was followed by the two enraged women.

People in cars began to honk encouragement as the drama unfolded in front of them. And on the opposite side of the street, a block behind, she saw Michel's gunman turn the corner, take one look in their direction, and instantly join the chase.

Maybe she should have sacrificed a little of the character of her part, Mariel reflected. No one ever ran the four-minute mile in three-inch stilettos, she was pretty sure of that.

The cat burglar caught up with her, grabbed her arm and kept running. This caused the hookers to scream like wounded banshees, but a glance showed her they at least were losing interest in the chase. Maybe she had crossed the frontier of their territory now.

The man with the gun, which he was now obviously holding in the pocket of his sweats, wasn't losing interest. He was pounding along, barely a block behind.

Fortunately, her car was around the next corner. Breathless, Mariel could only point wildly to the right as they approached the next street. The cat burglar understood and, keeping his grip on her arm, half dragged her into the turn.

Her car was halfway along the narrow, dark street. Mariel reached for her backpack, then gave vent to a breathless screech.

"What?" said the stranger.

"My bag!" she panted. "I left—my bag—no—no—keys!"

"Where?"

"In the—office," Mariel croaked.

Luck, she had called it? Where was the luck in escaping if Michel knew who had been there?

Three

They had slowed their steps, but now they heard the sounds of running footsteps behind them, and the stranger grabbed her arm again and set off across the street at an angle. She just saw the shadow of the mouth of the alley before they were in it.

It was pitch-dark, and their entry was the trigger for some frantic scuffling near some piles of refuse. Mariel hoped it wasn't rats.

The cat burglar seemed to have eyes as good as his namesake, because he led her safely through the alley past all impediments before her own eyes had become accustomed to the darkness. When they got to the other end a glance behind showed them the gunman framed at the entrance. A moment later they heard clanging and cursing, so his eyes weren't as good as the stranger's, either.

They crossed another narrow street and plunged into

another laneway. They were in a very old part of the city, the walls all worn, dark brick, the streets twisting and narrow. But the other, though he wasn't gaining, managed to stick on their tail.

Mariel was panting heavily when the stranger dragged her into another narrow opening. Now she could hear a pounding like thunder. The drum of doom, she thought a moment later. Because this time the lane led into a cramped courtyard, and there was no other exit.

"Oh my God!" Mariel panted. "Is there a fire esc—"

A sound from the stranger silenced her. He was staring around in the darkness, and now pressed his finger lightly to her lips. "This way," he whispered in her ear.

It was only then that she saw the little group of teenage boys clustered around a doorway, deep in shadow, murmuring amongst themselves. The stranger's confident hand clasped her wrist and drew her in that direction. Before Mariel had time to wonder, the door opened a crack, pushed from the inside, and music came pounding out.

The cat burglar leapt the last couple of feet and grabbed the door as the kids, glancing nervously at him, slipped through one by one. Mariel entered in their wake as the stranger held the door and prevented its closing. He followed her inside.

The music was loud and raucous, and that was nothing compared to the crowd. Mariel forgot all her troubles for a moment of wonder. Compared to what the women in here were wearing, her own outfit was a model of respectability. She had never seen so much big hair in her life, and the fingernails were longer than the skirts. And as for the eyes! Spiders were nothing to these women—most of them seemed to have tame lemurs on their lashes.

One or two of them were eyeing the stranger's snug black get-up with extremely frank approval. *"Chéri!"* said one, her popping eyes rivetted to his groin.

"He's a cat burglar!" Mariel told her waspishly. Since in French the phrase for *cat burglar* was *mount-in-the-air,* she received some wide-eyed looks of envy and approval.

"I believe you! *Comme elle a de la chance!"* a big, dark-eyed blonde cried, one wrist to her forehead in an excess of sensibility, faking a faint. "My dears!"

Mariel was starting to smell a rat.

But it was only when a clone from *The Wild Ones,* Marlon Brando from the black biker's cap down to the chain boots, groped her own butt, crying, "My God, you are so subtle! I love subtlety!" that the penny finally dropped.

"Thank you!" she muttered, as the cat burglar grabbed her hand again and started beating a path to the entrance door across the room.

"What are you drinking?" Brando shouted over the din.

"Scotch?" Mariel called hopefully, because she sure could use a drink.

Brando looked delighted. "I'll be right back! Wait for me! Don't disappear!"

She smiled helplessly at him as the stranger, still ruthlessly grasping her wrist, dragged her through the crush of dancing, gyrating male bodies.

"I'm pooped! Can't we stop for a quick drink?" she pleaded, as they arrived at the edge of the crowd a few feet from the door.

A large and burly bouncer was evicting the three

blue-jeaned kids who had entered through the back door
with them. "We only wanted to watch!" one was protesting.

The stranger stared at her disbelievingly. "A drink?"

"Marlon Brando over there offered me a scotch. I
sure could use something. And let's face it, the way
we're dressed, Michel would never find us in here."

He grabbed her wrist again without answering and
set off. The bouncer watched incuriously as they ran
out past him and up the steps of the areaway. They
emerged on a broad boulevard with plenty of traffic,
where a taxi screeched to a stop almost before the
stranger lifted his hand.

They scrambled in, and Mariel fell back against the
upholstery, half panting, half laughing. It was only as
she heard the stranger murmur "Le Charlemagne" that
she realized she had missed the moment for separating.
They ought to have said goodbye and each taken a separate cab.

"Is that your address?" she asked.

"But of course," he said, so blandly she didn't know
whether to believe him.

"I think we should separate now," she said, though
her heart wasn't in it. As the lights of Paris flickered
past, light and shadow falling over their faces in a
strange tempo, she gazed into his face and felt suddenly
that she was in a dream. A dream she had dreamt a
thousand times before without ever quite remembering.

"Separate?" he repeated, in soft protest. "Ah, no,
ma petite, I cannot be separated from you yet." He bent
over her, where she lay slouched down against the cush-
ions, his face close. Her pulse hammered a protest. She
lifted a hand to his chest, whether to hold him off or

draw him closer, even she didn't know. His lips moved closer.

"Stay with me tonight," he murmured.

This was the handsomest man in the world talking to her. Mariel's heart did a shaky back flip. Lust struggled with common sense, which reminded her that she didn't even know his name. And that he might well be in the enemy camp. *My enemy's enemy is my friend,* her heart protested, but common sense told her she couldn't be certain that he *was* Michel's enemy.

"I think I should get out," she murmured, half to herself. "Driver—" she called, but the stranger put his fingers to her lips to silence her.

"Where will you go?"

"Home, of course."

He shook his head. "Without your handbag? Where are your keys?"

"The landlady will let me in, and I have a spare key hidden."

"What besides your keys was in the bag?"

She was trying to remember where she had left the bag. She ran over those moments in the office—she had been picking up her bag when she noticed the open door of the secret office. And she had gone to close the office door. Had she left the bag on her desk, or taken it with her and dropped it in her scuffle with the stranger?

If she had left it on her desk there was just a faint possibility that Michel might think she had left her bag behind when she left for the night. If she had dropped it in his secret office...

She shook her head. "Just what you'd imagine. My credit cards, money...address book, phone numbers—everything."

What a fool. And all because she had fallen for a face

in a photograph. If she hadn't had complete brain collapse and decided to print that photograph, none of it would have happened. She would probably have been out of the office before the man even arrived.

Haroun watched her. He was aware of too many contradictions. Why was Michel Verdun chasing a lady of the night with an armed man in tow? What had she been doing in his office if she wasn't there at his invitation?

"And what of this man? When he finds your handbag with your address—will he make you a visit?"

Mariel shivered. Not before she had gathered her belongings and disappeared, she hoped. She had money in the flat. She would take her things to a hotel and phone Hal for instructions.

He noted the shiver. "What were you doing there?" he demanded.

She looked up at him through ridiculously long lashes, her eyes wary, challenging, but still somehow seductive and, as he expected, parried. "What were you?"

He laughed and lifted a hand, palm facing her, in a sign of surrender. *"Eh bien, d'accord!"* he said. "We ask no personal questions. Do you think the gun was for me or for you?"

He was looking at her with a devil-may-care glint in his eyes and tilt to his lips that made her heart kick again. She pressed her own lips together and lowered her head.

"I don't know. You can't have tripped the alarm, because I turned it off. Maybe he's had something new installed I don't know about."

His eyebrow went up. "You are familiar with his operation?"

"No personal questions, remember?"

''When you saw me, you said, *It's you*. And then, *Michelle is sick, so if you don't mind briefing me*—''

He looked at her enquiringly, but she only shook her head. He frowned in thought. ''Michel!'' he exclaimed, looking enlightened. ''Ah! I imagined Michelle was a girl you replaced, but you meant—Verdun himself. You thought I was there to meet Verdun, you were playing for time, is that right?''

She pressed her lips together and looked at him. Everything about him seemed to have a glow. His dark eyes, his waving hair, his warm skin. His whole being.

When she made no answer he went on thinking aloud. ''And yet you were there to...''

He paused invitingly. They were driving further away from her own *arrondissement* as they talked. She came out of a kind of daze to realize she was still half lying against the upholstery and he was still bent over her in intimate closeness. Mariel pushed the stranger aside and sat up with a small tug of regret for the loss of the sensual little cocoon she had been inhabiting.

''I want to go home,'' she said. ''Would you mind paying...?''

''No emergency funds tucked into the top of your stocking?'' he asked with a teasing smile, his finger tracing designs on her knee as she pretended not to be affected by the chills charging through her blood and reproved him with a look. ''But no—no stockings at all.''

''I've got to go home,'' she repeated. She leaned forward and murmured the name of a landmark near her apartment, and the driver pulled into a turn with an easy shrug.

It would be safe enough as long as she didn't let the stranger know her exact address, and she wouldn't be there past tonight anyway. The stranger wasn't a man who would feel the loss of fifty francs, not if he was calling Le Charlemagne home.

"And are we never to see each other again?" he continued, in a tone that wrenched at her heart.

Of course he didn't mean it. And neither did she—it had been just a crazy moment when she thought she had fallen in love with the photograph.

The photograph! Mariel bit her lip. She hadn't thought about that....

"What is it?" he murmured, noting her sudden change of mood, the delicious way her white teeth caught her lower lip as she looked at him. "You have changed your mind? You will come with me?"

Should she warn the stranger about the fact that Michel had been sent his photograph? But she knew nothing about him or his motives, another part of her argued. She couldn't tell him about the photo without exposing some part of her work. Suppose the stranger were actually in league with Michel, but double-crossing him? She now had to engage in damage limitation, and keep from Michel any clues as to who she was working for and how and what information she had been getting. She had to avoid anything that would confirm a suspicion that Hal Ward had got access to his top-secret computers.

For all she knew, the whole thing had been a setup. Maybe Michel had been clocking her visits for weeks. Maybe he had sent the stranger to pretend to be breaking in, too. Then followed it up with a raid, forcing her into the same camp as the stranger, making him an ally.

But still she felt guilty, not saying anything.

"Anyway," she murmured aloud, "it's all your fault I'm in this predicament."

"C'est vrai," the stranger replied, with a warm look. "So it is up to me to take care of you, no?"

And always that devil in his eyes, a look that made her shiver with delight. *In a life with him you'd always be laughing,* her heart suggested.

"I don't think it works that way," she said mildly.

"Si," he contradicted her. *"Tu verras."*

And she did see, sooner than either of them could have expected. On his way to the landmark she had named, the taxi driver took the usual route along the street where she lived, and as they passed the small, charming nineteenth-century building with blue shutters and blue wrought iron, she saw a car parked right in front of it. She sat up with a jerk, staring across the stranger's relaxed body out the window. Michel's car, she saw, as they drew close enough to read the plate.

A man sat at the wheel, smoking. He glanced over into the taxi just as the streetlight illumined the interior.

"Dieu!" Mariel murmured, and to recover from her unprofessional behaviour—she should never have stared out the window like that—tilted her head as if to kiss the stranger.

His arms instantly encircled her and he looked delighted. "Ah, you have had a change of heart, *ma petite,"* he observed, his lips close and parting hungrily.

"That's one of Michel's operatives in that parked car back there," she whispered, her mouth barely an inch from his. With extreme reluctance, since she liked being right where she was, she lifted her head to peer through the back window.

"Is he following us?" the stranger asked from beneath her, amusement still threading his voice. His closeness tickled her throat and made her yearn.

The car stayed where it was. "No," she murmured.

"Do you think someone is right in my fl—?" she began, then gasped as, one hand on her back, the other on her head, the stranger pulled her down.

Suddenly he was kissing her, with an expertise that exploded into sugared sweetness all through her body. Sensation seemed to arise from nowhere to engulf her, drowning her so that she could not resist.

There had never been a kiss like it since the beginning of the world, Mariel thought dreamily, letting herself sink down against him. She thrilled as his arms tightened possessively around her, his kiss becoming hungrier, more demanding.

Her hands went to his face, her fingers slipping around his neck, as all her blood sang with delight. It was the kiss she had dreamed of, a kiss to die for, her fogged brain murmured, her body promised. It was the cake she could both have and eat.

It was a once-in-a-lifetime kind of kiss.

"Et maintenant, mes enfants, où irions-nous? La Tour d'Eiffel?"

They surfaced to discover themselves in front of the monument Mariel had named, the driver calmly slipping a Gauloises between his lips as he tolerantly watched them over the seat back. The meter was still ticking.

The stranger smiled, touched her lips with a tender finger, and murmured, "Verdun's car was parked at your address?"

She nodded.

"Well, then, you can't return there, it is too dangerous. You must trust yourself to me now."

Since for the moment she really could see no other option, Mariel was silent. The stranger lifted his head. *"Le Charlemagne, s'il vous plait,"* he said again.

With an expressively Gallic shrug, the driver lifted a

cheap plastic lighter to his cigarette, flicked it to flame, drew deep, tossed it down onto the seat beside him, put the car in gear, and set it rolling.

"You really live in Le Charlemagne?" she asked, even more curious now about his reasons for breaking in to Michel's office.

The stranger misunderstood. "Yes. There is little reason for Verdun to know my face, even if he saw me long enough for recognition, which I am sure he did not. The office was, in any case, nearly dark. So I think we will be safe enough there."

The thought of the print of the photograph she had dropped somewhere surfaced in her mind. She wondered what Michel would make of it. It was proof that someone had broken in to his computers, but he must be wondering why anyone would have taken a hard copy.

"In spite of our no-questions policy it may be that the time has come for us to move on a step in intimacy," the stranger remarked, interrupting her train of thought. "What is your name?"

She hesitated. "Emma. What's yours?"

"Emma," he repeated. "A charming name. And I am called...Fred."

Four

Le Charlemagne was the name of a world-famous Rue de Rivoli shopping complex with fabulous shops on two levels. Above were seven floors of exclusive apartments. Overlooking the Jardin des Tuileries and the Seine, it was one of Paris's very exclusive addresses.

The concierge watched with benign interest as the pair strode along the concourse towards the bank of private lifts. The lift Fred led her to gave access to the garage, main, mezzanine and ninth floors only. He used a plastic key, and when they arrived at the top they stepped into a vestibule where a guard sat in front of a small bank of TV screens. Behind him was the open door of a small kitchenette.

Mariel's skin bumped with nerves as Fred greeted the man in Arabic, and she wondered if she had been wise to jump out of the frying pan with the stranger. He led her to the big double doors into the main apartment, while the guard's gaze followed them with a mixture of heavy disapproval and sexual curiosity marking his face.

Catching his eye, Mariel winked at him. The man blushed and dropped his eyes. Fred, noticing his reaction, looked from the guard to Mariel with a deadly little glint in his eyes that promised to make her pay for that one, and she couldn't stop the little expectant shiver that coursed over her skin in response.

Then they stepped across the threshold into a large, luxurious, oak-floored room, glowing with soft light, drapes open to expose a wall of glass that gave onto a wide terrace and a view of the lights along the Seine. The furnishings were in leather and a variety of rich and exotic woods polished to a gleam.

The predominant feeling was comfort. Mariel heaved a sigh and rubbed the back of her neck as some of the tension of the past couple of hours left her.

Fred nodded approvingly. "Safe now," he said, and turned as a manservant appeared on silent feet. "Evening, Mansour," he said cheerfully. "Will you ask Salma to show Madame to the ruby bedroom and see to any needs she has? Then I think we could both eat a little supper in—half an hour?"

He cocked an eyebrow at Mariel, who nodded gratefully. A moment later she followed an equally silent woman along a hall and into a beautifully furnished bedroom with ivory walls and rich red hangings. A king-size bed sat against the middle of one wall, surrounded by a dark wood floor topped by a luscious Persian carpet.

Salma stepped across the room to press a button and draw the magnificent ruby-coloured drapes that covered more windows onto the terrace.

"You desire a bath, Madame?"

That was exactly what she desired. "Please."

The woman opened a closet and lifted out a cream silk dressing gown and slip, which she carefully laid on the wide bed.

"Please make use of anything you need," Salma said graciously, in only slightly accented French, before disappearing through a door to the left. After a moment Mariel heard the sound of gushing water.

There was a dressing table opposite the foot of the bed, in front of the windows. She sank down onto the stool, stripping off the brassy wig to reveal her own crop of dark brown hair. She tossed the wig to one side and began carefully peeling off the false eyelashes on her upper and lower lids. There was a wastepaper basket under the dressing table, and into it she threw the wig and eyelashes. This was a disguise she wouldn't be using again.

There were several jars and bottles on the table and she wiped off the heavy makeup with relief. She unzipped the black suede boots and kicked them off, then stood and stripped.

Salma came back into the room again in a waft of steam and perfume and paused for a moment of surprise, quickly suppressed, as Mariel, tying the belt of the too-large dressing gown around her, moved towards her.

"Your bath is ready, Madame."

"I knew it," said Ash. "There was bound to be trouble."

Haroun had showered and washed his hair and was lounging on a sofa in a quilted black silk kimono open over his bare chest, black silk pyjama bottoms, and bare feet. He had the phone to his ear and was absently nibbling on some olives that Mansour had left at his elbow.

"You wouldn't call it trouble, exactly, if you could see her."

Ash made an impatient noise. "It's the fact that Vivian's seen you which is the trouble." *Vivian* was their code for Verdun. Ever since the disastrous leak over the Rose they had been much more circumspect on the phone. "We'd better double the guard on—"

"He didn't see my face for more than a few seconds, and most of that I spent chopping his hired muscle. I doubt—"

"Will you listen to yourself?" Ash interrupted. "Your face is not unknown. Your picture must have been in the paper half a dozen times this past year during the Barakat trade negotiations. It's a small leap, and Vivian is just the man to make it. Why else would you be covertly entering his office?"

"Ash, you're stiff-necked. You'll be fine once you're on the throne, it'll suit you then, but frankly at the moment you're boring me. We got away and the only clue left behind was her handbag, and there is no connection between us, right? Man would have to be a genius to realize the two of us broke in independently on the same night, for two different reasons."

"If you did. You have no idea why she was there, you said it yourself. You don't know who she's working for. How do you know she's not one of Vivian's own agents?"

Harry popped another olive and chewed reflectively. "Lighten up, Ash," he begged. "The worst aspect of this fiasco tonight is that I missed my chance to find out where the Rose is now. So where do I go from here? I've got some id—"

"The first thing you do," Ash interrupted harshly, "is get that woman out of the apartment. You think General Gordon isn't bright enough to use sex as a means—"

General Gordon was their code name for Ghasib, the Supreme President of Bagestan.

"And how did the estimable general know where I would be tonight?"

"We already know there's a leak somewhere. For God's sake, Haroun, don't get involved with her on any level. You can't risk it. She may be an assassin."

Much as he hated to admit it, his brother was right. He couldn't risk it. Harry sighed for the loss of what had promised to be a night to remember. "You don't know what you're asking, Ash. All right, you win."

"*Alhamdolillah,*" Ash exclaimed dryly.

"But as for the Rose—ah, gotta go," he interrupted himself quickly, as the door opened and Emma appeared.

Emma smiled and wiggled her fingers and moved over to the open door and onto the terrace, where Mansour had set a candlelit table with their meal. Haroun watched her pass almost open-jawed. Gone was the bunch-breasted, sassy-hipped redhead, and in her place was a graceful brunette, trailing the flowing silk of the too-long robe behind her.

"Is that her?" Ash demanded. "You sound like a man going into trance, Harry. Be careful. *She may be an assassin.*"

Following her with his eyes, Harry scarcely heard what his brother was saying.

On the terrace, Mariel stood looking out over the lights of the city. If she had thought Fred was handsome before, he was absolutely devastating here in his own home, wearing rich black silk that made him look like a sultan or something. He had showered but not shaved, and the beard shadow gave his eyes an even more devilish cast. Never in her life had she lost her heart so thoroughly to a total stranger—or to anyone!—but it would be insanity to think anything could come of it, so she had better find a way to get her heart back.

She shook herself out of dreams and into the here and now. Although it was late, there was still the noise of steady traffic below. Tomorrow was August first, and everybody was leaving Paris for the month. A lot more than usual would be taking their cars, no doubt, because of the threatened air traffic controllers' strike.

She was thinking over what she had overheard Fred say as she entered the room. "...*quant à la rose.*" ...*as for the rose.* Funny to be talking about flowers.

Fred slipped silently up behind her, not touching her, his hands gripping the railing on either side of her own. She felt his body warm the luscious silk she was wearing till it was a kiss on her skin, and pressed her lips together, praying for the strength to resist. She knew he was waiting for her to turn around into his embrace, and the knowledge ignited a nearly irresistible fire in her blood.

She knew nothing about him. The sooner she got away from him the better.

She would stay here tonight, but that didn't mean she was spending the night in his bed. And yet, if he made a real move, if he tried to make love to her—she knew she would find it impossible to resist. She was at her limit already. She dropped her head forward and stared down at the park.

Ash was right, Harry told himself—her presence was too strange, too much of a mystery. He couldn't risk acting on any assumption that she was the woman of pleasure she had first seemed. Yet he'd never met a woman before who exerted such a powerful physical draw on him. What a pity to waste it. He could control the urge to draw her hair aside and brush his lips against the back of her neck—just—but if she turned and offered him her mouth…impossible to resist her.

They stood in suffocating silence for a long moment.

"Shall we eat?" Harry murmured at last, lifting his hands and slipping them into the pockets of his kimono.

"Thank you," Mariel whispered, struggling for a normal tone, and waited till he had stepped away before she dared to turn. He was holding the chair for her, and she slipped into it with a smile that trembled only slightly.

"We will serve ourselves," Haroun said. He had told Mansour he wouldn't be needed, a move he now half regretted. But he lifted the chafing dish and offered her some of the concoction in it and she accepted with a determined little smile.

The night was warm and seemed perfumed as they ate the delicious little meal and chatted about food and the world and anything except what was uppermost on both their minds.

"May I use your phone after dinner?" Mariel asked once. "I must arrange to get some money."

He frowned. "I am happy to give you whatever money you require," he said.

She shook her head, trying to smile. "Thank you, but it's not necessary. I need enough to tide me over till I can get new bank cards and things." Hal would probably want her to fly back to California immediately. But that wouldn't be possible without her passport, and it would take time to get a replacement if she reported it lost or stolen.

Maybe she could think of some way of getting into her apartment. She eyed Fred speculatively. A cat burglar, if that was really what he was, would be of inestimable value in such a venture, but...

"I'll phone my...a friend and ask him to wire some."

This refusal irritated Harry, and the knowledge that this was so irritated him even more. What had she interrupted herself saying? *Mon ami?* Was that why she was resisting the attraction between them?

"Tell me what you were doing in Verdun's office tonight," he demanded harshly.

She looked at him. Her eyelashes and eyebrows were dark, so that her eyes, set above strong, sloping cheekbones, dominated her face. Her eyes were almond shaped, slightly slanted, a soft jade green, like a cat's, and equally assessing. Her richly toned brown hair was a very chic near-shoulder-length cut, with wings at her ears that emphasised the cheekbones.

She had wiped off her makeup and, as far as he could tell, hadn't replaced it. Her lips were a very kissable pink, her pale skin flawless.

If he let her walk out of his life he might not be able to find her again. He had clocked the street and even the building where she had seen Verdun's car, but what good was that if she never went back there? If she had rented it under a false name?

"Why should we not compare notes?" he demanded, when she remained silent. "Perhaps we can be of help to each other."

She gazed levelly at him, pursing her delicious mouth a little. "You know that's not possible. We don't know

what each of us wants, and until we do, we can't afford
to say anything."

"If we don't tell each other we will never know,"
he countered.

She lifted her hands. "Exactly. A vicious circle."

He could see the curve of her breast in the neckline
of the robe. For a moment he had the feeling that that
quintessentially feminine sight was more important than
anything else in the world, that everything else was
nothing but games. But the thought was impossible to
express in words, and anyway, it surprised him, made
him slightly uncomfortable with himself.

She might be an assassin. Nothing was too low for
Ghasib, of course, but that would make it a very sophisticated operation. It would mean his conversation
with Ash had not been secure. And then, that someone
had devised the ruse of putting an agent into Verdun's
office in the guise of another burglar. What easier way
to get past someone's trust barrier?

His gaze searched Emma's face. She was hiding
something, without a doubt. But was it a murderous
intent? A knife, a poison capsule?

Haroun jumped to his feet, drawing the cat eyes up
to his, and came around the table towards her. "Stand
up!" he commanded.

Mariel's heart leapt painfully as he reached for her.
One hand grasped her wrist with a firmness of purpose
that hurt, the other dragged her chair back. She straightened, blood pounding wildly up into her head, making
her dizzy.

He pulled open the dressing gown, slipped his hands
inside, found the plain silk sheath of the cream night-
dress. His hands ran hard and firm down her back from

shoulder to waist over the silk, and her blood went suddenly hot.

"Stop it," she protested, in a scratchy, hoarse voice, as the heat burnt up to melt her.

"I apologize, Emma, but too many of my family have died at the hands of assassins. I do not care to go the same way." He smiled, showing her his teeth. "Not yet."

It took a moment for the words to sink in, and meanwhile his hands were running over her full, firm breasts, noting the suddenly peaked nipples with only a clenching of his jaw, down her arms, to her hips, bottom, thighs, inner thighs, legs.

She looked down at him crouching at her feet, all the building sexual excitement his touch evoked transmogrifying into furious indignation.

"*What?*" Mariel demanded, in a kind of growled screech.

It was the work of moments. He was already standing straight again, and his hands were in her hair, his fingers prodding every inch of her scalp, as if she might have a poison capsule taped to a lock of hair.

She backed off a step and slapped his hand angrily away.

"Who the hell do you think you are?" she snapped.

"It must be done. I have not checked your robe."

"And you're not going to!"

"Yes," he said. The flame between them now was changed, but it still licked heat over them. He stepped towards her, and she jerked back.

"You are not going to touch me again!" she vowed. She lifted her hands and stripped off the silky robe, balled it up and threw it at his head. Then she stood like a statue, cold and condemning, as he searched the pockets and cuffs, ran the seams and hem through his fingers.

He was aware of her body, smoothly muscled and firm, and naked save for the light silk of the nightgown. He noted how the silk caressed her low, rounded hips, clung to her pubic hair, outlined her nipples, folded at her feet so that only her toes were visible. He could even see the shadow of the butterfly tattoo on her abdomen, so thin was the fabric.

The green eyes were icy with indignant rage. He had probably ruined his chances with her forever, and he cursed Ash for his paranoia, which was so contagious.

The search of the robe took only a minute, and he held it open at the neckline, offering it to her. But she disdained to let him help her with it, instead pulling it from his grasp with a look that would have frozen marble. She slipped her hands back inside and tied the waist with a snap.

"Now," she said, "since suspicion seems to be in the wind, perhaps you won't object if I search you for signs of murderous intent?"

If there hadn't been so much tension in the air, he might have laughed. Instead he inclined his head and held his arms out from his sides, like someone who has set off the metal detector at the airport.

She did a professional job, he noted, starting at the neck and working methodically out along the tops of his arms, back in underneath. Her hands then moved inside his kimono to his armpits, his bare chest, around his back, down to his waist.

She found the mobile phone in the pocket of his kimono and, tossing it onto the table, returned to her task.

He felt the stirring of his flesh as her hands ran around the waistband of his pyjama bottoms and slid down over his buttocks, and as she bent her knees and sank down to where her mouth was on a level with his groin, it leapt to full attention.

It was impossible to miss the fact of his arousal through the black silk. Mariel gritted her teeth against the answering melting of her own body, and flattened her hands on his thigh.

"If you touch me anymore I will not be responsible for the consequences," he warned.

Her hands twitched instinctively away, but she resolutely replaced them. "I am searching you for a gun," she insisted between her teeth, as the betraying flush crept up into her cheeks. She drew her hands quickly down one leg to his ankle, and then repeated the motion on the other. Meanwhile his hungry sex threatened to burst the silk.

His hands caught her shoulders as she straightened, and held her tight as they stared into each other's eyes.

"We are moths," he said. "Drawn by the flame that we cannot resist."

Mariel licked her lips, and gazed hungrily into his handsome face, saying nothing. She was being a fool. She knew she was being a fool. But it was so delicious.

He leaned towards her damp, willing lips.

The mobile on the table rang shrilly. His mouth inches from hers, Harry stiffened and closed his eyes. It rang again. It could only be Ash on this phone, and if he didn't answer it he knew damned well the guard outside would come thundering through the door within a minute.

With a curse, he dropped his hands from her shoulders and reached out to pick it up.

"*Baleh.*"

"It's the last day of the month. I forgot to give you the new phone numbers," said Ash.

He was pretty sure that wasn't the reason Ash had called. His brother was nothing if not psychic.

"Right," he said.

"Are you ready?"

Haroun strode over to the balcony, looking out over the river and breathing for calm. "Go ahead."

He coded the replacement numbers into the mobile's memory as Ash dictated. It was one of many precautions insisted on by Najib, who oversaw their security. New numbers every month for all their phones, including this one. He keyed in the code to alter his own number as Ash read it out, then said goodbye.

"Keep the lid on," Ash advised, and hung up.

Emma, he saw, had returned to her seat and was attacking the mouthwatering dessert that was Salma's specialty.

He grinned at her, that devilish grin, and Mariel had to look away. *"Revenons à nos moutons..."* he said invitingly. *Getting back to our sheep,* or *Now, where were we?*

"Our sheep were all the wrong kind," she reminded him. "They are better off straying."

She was right, of course. But he wished she were not so easily able to be pragmatic. "You and my brother have a lot in common," he remarked, indicating the phone.

"Who is your brother?" she asked, and wondered why that made his face go tight. He slipped the phone into his pocket and strode over to the serving trolley, where he set a little silver pot on a flaming ring.

"Coffee?"

She nodded, and they waited in loaded silence until

he had poured two tiny cups of rich, dark Turkish coffee, which they drank in silence. When they finished he held up the little pot enquiringly. She nodded and watched him refill the little cup. Then she glanced up. "If I could use your phone now?"

He waved his hand to indicate the apartment. "You can see that I will have no problem with any sum you might need. If you prefer, we can call it a loan."

But she couldn't take money from him when it might have come from Ghasib or Michel....

"If I could use it in private?"

There was a flicker in his dark eyes. He stared at her gravely. "I'm afraid that will not be possible."

Well, perhaps it was too much to expect. "Are your lines tapped?" she asked.

He laughed. "Not so far as I know. But who can be sure in this age? Even this conversation may be overheard."

Mariel involuntarily glanced around. There was nothing opposite the balcony except the Tuileries Gardens and the river and the city beyond. They were sitting at the centre of the balcony, which ran the whole length of the building. They seemed in a world apart, remote from the buildings on either side. It was a warm, clear night and the lights of the city did not entirely wipe out the stars overhead.

Fred stood and went to a small cabinet further along the terrace. He opened a door and took out a cordless phone which he brought to her and, with a little bow, set down in front of her before returning to his seat opposite. She eyed him speculatively. He calmly returned her gaze and she decided he was immovable on this point.

A breeze caressed her as she picked up the receiver.

Important numbers were coded into her cellphone and recorded in her address book, both of which were gone. But fortunately she had one number committed to memory—the special phone in Hal Ward's private office.

"Yes," said his voice.

"This is Emma," she said in English. She had to assume Fred spoke English, but he couldn't have known she did. It was a pity to give away such an advantage, but Hal didn't speak very good French and she had to be sure he knew exactly what was happening. "How are things with you?"

She could hear his ears prick up at her use of the code to indicate that things weren't right with her.

"Emma. Is this line clean?"

"Not sure. I lost my bag tonight and I need money. I was, uh…doing overtime tonight…."

Quickly and carefully, partly in double speak and partly straight, she outlined what had happened, including the news that she was now at the apartment of the stranger whose photograph was in the files she had copied to him tonight.

When she had finished, Hal Ward said, "Is this guy okay?"

"I don't know. He seems to suspect me of being a hit woman."

She showed Fred her teeth. He laughed.

"Seriously?"

"He just searched me."

There was a pregnant pause. "You be careful, Em. Any chance of your getting out of there tonight? I could arrange with a hotel…."

"I can't go to a hotel without a *carte d'identité.*"

"Damn, I forgot. What about reporting your bag as lost to the police?"

"Dressed like a hooker," she reminded him.

"I don't like the sound of this," her cousin said. "You be careful. I'll wire you some money so you can pick it up with no ID. The important thing is to get out of town. The air traffic controllers went on strike in France as of midnight your time. I know there's an Amtravel foreign exchange office in the Gare de Lyon. Can you get down there?"

She hated the thought of giving up her investigations before they were complete, but it had been her own stupid mismanagement, and there was no point in arguing. She was a liability now.

"Yes, I can walk that far."

"All right, I'll send the money to be picked up without ID. Get down there as soon as they open in the morning, get the cash and take the first train you can get. Don't go to your father's or anyone you know—if Verdun's got your address book they'll be able to track you. Just get out of town and into a hotel where you can lie low for a few days. Let me know as soon as you've done that."

She made a mental note that she would have to report to the police in whatever town she arrived in that her handbag had been stolen on the train while she was asleep, in order to get a temporary *carte d'identité*.

"I won't be in the office over the weekend, so call me on my cellphone. Call me every twelve hours, as close to noon and midnight my time as you can. That's what—nine a.m. and nine p.m. Paris time."

"You'll have to give me the number. I lost all my stuff in my handbag. Wait a sec while I get a pen."

She set down the phone and got to her feet. Fred waved her to a pen and notepad on the cabinet and she returned to the table.

When it was all arranged, and with warnings from her cousin ringing in her ears, she hung up. After a moment she finished the last of the Turkish coffee in her cup. The dark, thick grounds, which Gypsies read fortunes in, slithered back down into the cup as she watched, and took on the unmistakable shape of a guillotine.

Five

Mariel tore off the scrap of paper with the phone number and tucked it into her pocket. Fred got to his feet and, a little like a jailer, waited for her to precede him into the lounge.

It was a lovely room. She stood looking around. Fred picked up an Arabic newspaper and sank down onto the luxurious leather sofa under the glow of the room's only lamp.

It was a warm night. A soft breeze blew in through the doors, bringing the scent of the flowers on the terrace, the sound of a horn below, the glow of the city and the stars.

It was all very intimate and inviting. She could almost imagine that she had the right to take a magazine and lie down on the sofa, her head in his lap.

Lady, shall I lie in your lap? No, my lord.
No.

The heat rising in her cheeks, Mariel bent over the table opposite him and flipped through a stack of magazines and newspapers.

"May I take a few of these to read?"

His eyes found hers. "You do not expect to sleep?"

"Do you?" she countered dryly.

Fred shrugged. "Take whatever you like. But you have nothing to fear from me."

"Snap," she said.

They were too tense to smile at the stupidity of it. Mariel picked up a few magazines at random, said a stiff good-night, and went back to the ruby bedroom, where she tossed them on the bed. She found there was a lock on the door, so she turned it, as Hal had advised, and for good measure pushed a large stuffed chair against it. Then she checked the lock on the sliding door to the terrace.

She climbed into bed at last, all her instincts at war in her. One part of her said she could trust Fred, another said she might be murdered in her bed. One demanded she get close to him, while another suggested that if she spied on him she might hear some clue.

Her body cried out for the nearness of his.

She was going to ignore them all and try to get some sleep. But that wouldn't happen yet. She was far too wide awake. Mariel picked up the latest *Hello!* magazine from the little pile and hoped it would have a soporific effect.

Wedding In Paradise! read the headline over the photo of a man and woman smiling lovingly at each other. *After Five Years, A Reunion For Prince Najib And His Bride! Exclusive Pictures Of The Palace Wedding!*

She flipped to the photo spread. An Englishwoman

marrying an Arab prince, and in one of the most stunning wedding dresses Mariel had ever clapped eyes on. Prince Najib was Cup Companion to Prince Rafi of East Barakat, and more important, the magazine breathlessly informed her, the only one of the mysterious male heirs of the deposed Sultan of Bagestan to have been publicly revealed since 1972, when the entire family had gone into hiding.

Something in the prince's face reminded her of Fred, she thought lazily. Probably just her Westerner's eye. Maybe she just found it difficult to distinguish one Arab face from another. He certainly wasn't as handsome as Fred.

Or maybe she was just obsessed enough to see Fred's face in everything.

It was a romantic story, though. Together again after five years in which he hadn't remembered he had a wife and son....

She fell asleep between one thrilling caption and the next.

"I am sorry to disturb you at this hour. But tonight I have learned something that may be of crucial importance in our attempts to identify the al Jawadi heirs. I wonder if His Excellency is aware of the existence of something called the al Jawadi Rose."

Michel Verdun stiffened before the glittering smile that came into the other's eyes. "I am sure you mean the Bagestani Rose, Monsieur Verdun. We are of course aware of it. A priceless jewel stolen from the people of Bagestan by the al Jawadi thirty years ago when the corrupt regime was at last mercifully toppled by President Ghasib."

"Yes, of course, my mistake, the Bagestani Rose."

"What of it?"

"I have learned through my sources that the Rose has resurfaced. Apparently it was in the possession of the lost wife of Prince Najib all the time."

"Then it must be recovered from the lost wife of Prince Najib," said the other chillingly.

"Apparently it has already been removed from her home. We are not certain by whom, but we have a photograph of one who was seen at the woman's apartment shortly before it was reported to have been taken. I have it here."

He passed it over. The chargé d'affaires took it and glanced down without much apparent interest. Then his lips thinned in something like shock.

"This man has taken the Rose?" he grated, after a moment. "You are certain of this?"

The black gaze fixed him. Verdun's own eyes fell, though he struggled against the compulsion. "No, not certain—the men didn't actually see him pick up the Rose, of course. But there is a strong circumstantial case—and I believe the same man broke in to my own offices earlier tonight."

"Broke in to your offices? How can this be?"

"I believe one of my own employees assisted him."

Again that cold smile. "Your employee has been subverted by—?"

Verdun felt sweat on his back. "Not one who had access to anything of importance. She—"

"You are a fool to use a woman as anything other than a sexual pawn or an assassin. Women cannot be trusted. Their sexual passions dominate their thinking."

Verdun nodded apologetically. "Unfortunately my computer specialist resigned suddenly to take a job in America. Such experts are not easily found. Otherwise

I assure you women hold no positions of importance...."

"I will pass this photograph on."

"Perhaps you are not aware that this man is a Cup Companion to Prince—"

"It is no more than to be expected of the Barakati princes that they should harbour the al Jawadi."

Mariel awoke with sunlight filtering between the drapes, and lay in the huge bed for a moment, feeling somewhat daunted, taking stock. No home, no car, no clothes, no *carte d'identité,* no passport, no money. Little sleep. And accepting shelter from a man whose motives she had no insight into and whose good looks scrambled her brains.

Not a situation to wish on anyone. But she was alive, something she couldn't have guaranteed last night. And somehow a smile was playing on her lips, and underlying all her worry was a feeling of...anticipation.

When she realized this, Mariel snorted impatiently and flung back the bedclothes. Her watch read past eight o'clock. Time she was out of here. The Amtravel office at the Gare de Lyon must have opened at seven.

She had a quick, cool shower and dressed. Someone had laundered her underwear and top, and rubbed up the leather skirt and suede boots, but still she wished she had something different to wear. It wasn't going to be fun, walking all the way to the Gare de Lyon in broad daylight dressed like a *poule,* especially along the Rue de Rivoli, but the alternative was to borrow money from Fred for a cab, and...well, she'd rather not.

She picked up the scrap of paper with Hal's mobile number on it and slipped it carefully into the little pocket of the skirt, then pulled the chair away from the inner door and unlocked it. But she went out the other way, onto the broad, sun-filled, terra-cotta-tiled terrace. Empty. She wandered to the corner of the building and peered around. Halfway along the next terrace, the same table they had eaten at last night was being set for breakfast. Mansour's back was turned to her as he worked.

"Bonjour," said a voice, and Mariel whirled. Wearing shorts, trainers, a towel around his neck, and little else, Fred came jogging along the deck towards her. He had worked up a good sweat, his skin was glowing like polished wood and his thick black hair flopped attractively over his forehead. He still hadn't shaved. He looked like an advertisement for an extremely expensive men's cologne.

"Bonjour," she returned, choking on her own heart.

"Sleep well?" She nodded. "Breakfast will be ready in a few minutes. Will you join me?" She nodded mutely again, and he carried on at an easy pace. She watched him go past Mansour and down around the next corner. Clearly he had another circuit to do.

"You arranged to get some money today?" Fred asked ten minutes later, as he spread a chunk of baguette liberally with the delicious country butter.

Mariel nodded, deciding it would be safe to tell him this much. "I have to go to the Gare de Lyon."

"You will want to go immediately after breakfast," he told her. "I will take you."

Mariel pressed her lips together. "There's no need for that."

"But of course! What if the money were to fail to arrive? What would you do then?"

Perhaps because her heart was at war with her decision, she found this argument impossible to resist. She nodded and bent her head, trying to stifle a smile. It was likely that he had an impersonal—even a hostile—reason for not wanting to lose track of her, but Mariel couldn't help the little burst of delight rippling through her. She didn't want to leave him until some definite connection had been made between them, something that would mean someday, somehow, they would get together again.

She didn't want to leave him at all.

It was almost another hour before they got up from the table and climbed into the elevator. They were a strange mismatch in their clothing. Fred wore sunglasses, a black polo shirt snug over his chest, casual sand-coloured pants and an expensive belt, a Gucci leather bag that held his phone and money, and bare feet in Gucci loafers. He looked wealthy and sophisticated, and an unlikely partner—in daylight, anyway—for the sexily thigh-booted Mariel. She supposed that would make them stand out, if there was anyone looking.

The elevator moved quickly down to the main floor. "There will be taxis out the door on the left," Fred said as the doors opened.

It was early, but there were plenty of people browsing in and out of the designer boutiques. All tourists, of course: any Parisian who hadn't left Paris last night would be leaving today. As Mariel stepped out of the elevator a woman turned to give her a head-to-toe examination, wondering if this was the latest Paris fashion, and she choked on a giggle, wondering if she would start a new trend in Japan and America.

Fred grabbed her arm and hissed her name just as she noticed three obviously Arab men a few yards away, pretending not to look in their direction.

Mariel was terrified. How had Michel found them so quickly? Fred cursed and dragged her back into the elevator. He rammed his card into the slot, banged the button, and the doors closed.

"We'll take the car," he said, as the elevator sank down and pinged. "Follow me." They stepped out into the garage and Fred took her wrist. "Left at the corner," he muttered.

But when they turned the corner two men in mechanic's overalls bending over a car halfway down the long row of gleaming cars glanced up with interest. Fred pulled her into an about-face and they strolled back around the corner and then raced to the elevator.

He jammed his card into the slot, but the doors didn't open. "It's gone back up!" He cursed. They could hear the sound of running footsteps. "This way!" Fred cried.

He led her up a ramp and past another long row of parked cars. At the end she could see a metal gate to the outside. Fred ran to a unit beside it and jammed his card in again, and the gate clanged and started up with agonising slowness.

"Go!" he called, and Mariel dropped to the dirty tarmac and rolled under the gate, getting covered in dirt in the process. Fred followed her. They got to their feet and tore up the sharp incline. At the top another metal gate was just opening, and they squeezed their way through that and set off down the narrow street it gave onto. "Left!" Fred cried as they neared an intersection, and Mariel hurled herself into a narrow, picturesque street. The sound of footsteps resounded from behind them.

They turned, and turned again. Mariel was starting to pant. Her high-heeled boots were a liability, and she knew Fred could have run much faster. They could still hear the sounds of pursuit. The men were getting nearer.

The next street they turned into was lined with shops and cafés on both sides. "In here!" Fred commanded, halfway along the row, and dragged her into a dark, overcrowded boutique with the name *Tribu* roughly painted on the window.

It was a small boutique, but there was room to hide. It was crammed with racks of old clothes and jewellery. She could see changing-room curtains at the back.

"Grab some clothes to try on!" she hissed.

There were two salesclerks, one guy and one girl, in the back of the shop, talking in low voices. They looked up and called, *"Bonjour, Monsieur, bonjour, Madame,"* then went back to their conversation.

Mariel, who was panting hard, left it to Fred to reply and went to the racks.

"Hi there," Fred said loudly in English. "Mind if we just sort of look around?"

"You are welcome," the girl answered in accented English. She was, Mariel noted belatedly, wearing a nose ring, purple hair, and a sheer green fifties night-gown that barely reached her thighs over a mouldy black bra and waist-high black briefs. Her boots and socks were black.

Mariel picked up a pair of jeans. They were old and worn and looked as if they had come out of an Oxfam shop. Well, things could be worse, she supposed. It might have been infants' wear. With one eye always on the window in the door, which gave the only access onto the sun-filled street, she quickly grabbed a few more items and moved to the back.

"Could I try these on, please?" she asked, following Fred's lead by speaking English.

She was examined up and down. "Sure," said the girl. She took the items from Mariel and led her to a curtained-off cubicle. "You are change your image, isn't it?" she noted.

"That's right," Mariel said.

"We 'ave everyzing 'ere. My boss, Gerard, 'e go to all the Oxfam and the old houses and 'e bring wonderful stuff."

Fred was talking to the male clerk. As Mariel closed the curtain she saw him being led into the cubicle next door. The male clerk was also a devotee of grunge. His head was naked except for an orange forelock, and he had a dagger tattoo above one ear, various pieces of pierced jewellery, a mass of pewter bracelets on both arms, a denim sleeveless jacket and camouflage combat pants.

"Thank you," Fred said in English.

"We have boots in your size, I sink. I will louk."

As she stripped, Mariel eyed what she had pulled from the racks. Almost anything would be better than what she was wearing, which was distinctive enough to enable the men to keep on their trail wherever they ran. But grunge? Wouldn't that be just a case of out of the frying pan?

They didn't have much choice now.

She slipped on a pair of torn bell-bottom blue jeans, the frayed holes held together in places with safety pins or mended with bits of coloured cloth. They rested on her hips below her navel, just revealing her butterfly tattoo and navel ring. Of the tops she chose a sleeveless blouse with a back closure and a Peter Pan collar, in rather yellowed white cotton. It ended above the waistband of the jeans, leaving two inches of her stomach bare.

So far, so good.

Outside, the two salesclerks were lazily discussing a music concert the boy had attended, when the girl suddenly hissed, "What do you think is going on with these two?"

"*Sais pas.*"

"Well, it's funny. Why does a guy like him want to dress grunge all of a sudden?" She sounded half-worshipful, as if Fred had felled her with one glance. Mariel could certainly empathize.

"*Sais pas.*"

"Do you think they are avoiding someone? They kept looking out the front. And did you see that one who looked in the door just now? He was very sinister. Do you think they are being chased?"

"You are too romantic," the boy said disparagingly.

Mariel felt goose bumps prickle her skin. So they were still out there. She pulled back the curtain and stepped out. The salesclerk was impressed by the transformation.

"It is very well," she said, reverting to English. "Very change, *non?* You want shoes?"

"Yes," Mariel said. "I want the whole thing."

"Sure, okay," the clerk said, then stopped where she was as Fred came out of the second cubicle. He was wearing green combat pants that looked as though they really might have seen combat, boots and a worn black T-shirt with the sleeves torn out, revealing his muscled upper arms. Mariel bit back nervous laughter. He suddenly looked like someone who broke all the rules. Dangerous.

The salesclerk stood blinking at him, hypnotized.

"You are going to a masquerade party?" the boy cleverly asked.

"Yes," Mariel began, just as Fred said, "We manage a rock group."

That got their attention. "Really? What band?" said the boy.

"It's an American group—we're launching in Europe. We just signed them," Fred said. Mariel smiled. Fred certainly could improvise. Maybe he really *was* someone who broke all the rules. She certainly had seen him break more than he obeyed. "You probably haven't heard of them yet," he said, with a self-deprecating shrug. "Surgical Procedure."

"But yes!" the girl cried, totally under his spell. "I am sure I heard that name." She turned to her partner. "You know this group!" she insisted. "An American group!"

Fred smiled approvingly at her while Mariel's fingers tensed with jealousy. "Well, that's great. You'll be hearing a lot more soon."

"Are you going to the festival next week in Fréjus?"

"Do you advise it?" Fred asked, with flattering attention.

"Oh, yes! Everyone is going to be playing there! It will be just like Glastonbury! If you—"

The girl quailed and fell silent, and only then did Mariel realize that she had glared a warning at her. She shook her head. She must be losing her mind.

"So you want the whole image?" the boy suggested. Fred nodded. "You need some piercing. We have the pierced look." He led them to a revolving rack, and chose a few items. "The studs work with magnets, and the rings just with tension. We have some tattoo-look transfers, too...."

Ten minutes later the two salesclerks were standing

back to admire their handiwork. "You look *très* cool. Very grunge. Only, you are a little too clean."

It was pretty impressive, as transformations went. They now sported nose jewellery, ear studs, and tattoos. Fred had an eyebrow ring. Mariel's navel ring and butterfly tattoo blended right in.

"Only for the 'air," suggested the girl dubiously.

"Wigs?" Mariel enquired.

"We don' do weeg. But the boutique beside us—it's a 'air boutique. They do lots of our clients. You can go right srough zat door."

"Oh, I don't know…" Mariel began, but stopped as Fred touched her arm with warning pressure. "Great," he said, smiling. He pulled a roll of cash out of his bag, peeled off a bunch of franc notes and laid them on the bill. "You've been a great help," he said, picking up the shopping bag which held their own clothes.

He led Mariel to the communicating door, then, as if in afterthought, turned. "Oh—I wouldn't like the media or the competition to get wind of the launch before we announce it," he told the wide-eyed kids. "They may have tailed us to Paris. Think you can keep your mouths shut about seeing us if anyone asks?"

They agreed with silent vigour, like two nodding dogs in a car going over a speed bump.

"They're patrolling the street out there," Fred muttered to Mariel, opening the connecting door. They stepped through into the opposite boutique and came out near a short row of sinks. This shop was twice the length of the one called Tribu, and seemed to back onto the next street.

Two men were getting their hair washed. Fred paused for a moment, staring towards the glass facade of the shop, orienting himself. "Okay, Emma," he said.

"With a little luck that door on the left leads out the back door onto the next street. Just head for it, don't turn if someone challenges us."

A woman came hurrying over. *"Bonjour, Madame, bonjour, Monsieur."*

Fred cursed under his breath. Someone spoke behind them and they turned.

The orange-thatched guru of grunge had come in behind them to beckon the woman over. "They want to complete their new look," he explained helpfully to the manageress. "You maybe have some appointments free this morning, Cecile?"

"But of course!" the manageress exclaimed.

In another moment they'd been robed and shrouded and each had their head in a sink.

"I don't like the smell of it," Hal Ward said. "This guy Verdun is mixed up with every vicious character on the planet. Just keep an eye on her. Try and get on her trail at Le Charlemagne. Put someone at the Gare de Lyon in case you miss her."

"Got it."

"Don't approach her unless she's in trouble—she won't thank you if you spoil her game—in which case take all necessary steps to protect her. I want to know she's safe, that's all."

"It definitely suits you," Mariel told Fred with mock enthusiasm, examining his sunflower-yellow dye job. They had escaped out the back door of the hairdressers' into a waiting taxi, and were en route for the Gare de Lyon. The traffic was terrible. "I love the black roots. It adds that touch of jaded sleaze so necessary to the well-turned-out punk rock manager."

It amazed her how much a couple of fake tattoos, a row of earrings and an eyebrow ring gave him the air of an anarchist. His two-day-old beard took on a different meaning, too.

Nothing disguised his glowing skin, his rippling muscles, and his good health, though. Or the sexual charisma that still emanated from him in too high a dose for her peace of mind. Her heart was clicking like a Geiger counter held over a mother lode of pure uranium.

"Mind you, it doesn't really go with the Gucci bag."

Fred lifted a hand to the two bunches of green hair messily tied just above her ears. Her eyes looked even greener now. The outfit gave her the look of a teenager, some middle class mother's spoiled, rebellious darling.

Fred frowned. "How old are you?" he demanded.

She laughed, throwing him a look, as a delicious tingle raced along her spine, and didn't answer.

Fred contented himself with giving her a lazy grin that made her go pink, then mercifully turned away. He flicked the shopping bag holding their old clothes.

"I can at least change my clothes at the station," he remarked with a grin. "But you will not wish to be so conspicuous—what will you do?"

"I'll buy something ordinary when I've picked up the money."

"And then where will you go?"

Her lashes dropped, hiding her eyes from him. "I'm not sure," she murmured, but when he said nothing, felt pressured to answer, "I'll get a hotel room, I guess."

She didn't mention that first she intended to get out of town.

"A hotel room?" he repeated. "What hotel?"

Mariel bit her lip, wishing she could tell him everything. Suddenly she understood how spies were undone by sex. Her brain had started malfunctioning the moment she met Fred.

"I...haven't decided."

He gazed at her with a probing look that made her restless. As if by looking into her eyes he could see her life projected on the screen of her soul.

"Emma," he said. "You know now that this is not a child's game. The stakes are very, very high, and there are more players than you know. If you are in league with my enemies you yourself will not escape, whatever the outcome. If you are an innocent bystander, you now share my own danger.

"You have the chance to confess, Emma. I have to know the truth about you," he said, with an urgency that rippled through her. "If you tell me the truth I can help you. I will look after you. Tell me the truth."

Six

At that moment the cab drew to a sudden stop behind a long line of cars waiting to turn into the Gare de Lyon. Ahead they could see chaos. "Won't get closer for half an hour," the driver remarked philosophically.

"We'll get out here," Fred said, handing over money. He opened the door as another car pulled up tight on Mariel's side of the car, hemming her in. With a shrug she scrambled across the seat, jumped out as he grabbed the bag of their clothes, and followed him down the street to the station entrance.

The place was bedlam. Cars were jammed in every direction, people were crawling over bumpers and heaving luggage across hoods and roofs. People shouted and called, babies screamed, horns honked.

"The strike!" Mariel exclaimed. "I forgot about the air traffic strike." By the look of this there wouldn't be a train seat available anywhere. The Gare de Lyon was the station for trains to the south, and today was August first. Half Paris would be trying to get to the Mediterranean this morning.

Inside the station they stood at the edge of a mass of humanity as if in the bait pot of some giant fisherman. The crowd seethed and roiled, moving in clusters and swells in the hall, and up and down the beautiful double staircase, as if the grand design lay in the swirling patterns of the whole mass rather than any individual purpose.

"How am I going to find the Amtravel office?" Mariel breathed.

"Let's look for the sign," Fred advised, but Mariel just grinned up at him. She was too short to see a thing beyond the shoulders of the people directly in front of her. "Come," he said, taking her hand and drawing her around along the perimeter of the concourse, where the crowd was thinner.

Mariel felt vulnerable in such a crowd, and was suddenly very glad Fred had insisted on coming with her. It was a long ten minutes before she found herself in front of the Amtravel office, but it would have taken her much longer by herself.

There, too, there was a lineup, and with a resigned shrug she joined it. Fred meanwhile found himself a pillar in front of the Amtravel office where he propped himself to wait, lazily watching the crowd, absorbed in his own thoughts.

There was no knowing what had led Ghasib's agents—as the men had to be—to Haroun al Muntazir, but they were certainly not interested in any mere Cup Companion to Prince Omar. It was clear that they suspected, or even knew, who he was.

Well, they had been prepared for the possibility ever since Ghasib's agents had got to the Rose before him. There was a leak somewhere, and as of this morning it was capable of doing very serious damage.

They had always thought that Ghasib might hold back from killing a known al Jawadi, for fear of repercussions in Bagestan. The people might riot if an heir of the old sultan was revealed, only to be murdered. But if he could kill one of them *before* he was publicly revealed, there might be much less political fallout.

He wondered if Emma was the source. No doubt he had been a fool to let her use the phone last night. Well, he wouldn't be the first man undone by a pretty face.

And if it *was* Emma's doing, he guessed it wouldn't be long before the men showed up here.

Haroun set the shopping bag between his feet and pulled out his phone. He pressed Ash's code and, seeing the unfamiliar number scroll onto the little screen, made a mental note to memorize the new numbers Ash had given him. If his phone crashed he'd be dead in the water.

He was waiting with the phone to his ear, his hand in his pocket toying with some change, when a beggar approached. ''Could you spare something towards a cup of coffee?''

When a beggar approaches you, give the first coin that comes to your hand when you put your hand in your pocket.

That was the old dictum, not so relevant now when a beggar risked getting only centimes, but Haroun had always had a kind of superstition about it. As it happened he had all the coins in his pocket—change from the taxi—cupped in his hand when the beggar spoke, and he simply drew it out and put them into the man's palm.

"Baleh," said Ash's voice, as the man thanked him. Haroun flicked him a salute and the beggar moved away.

"Ash!" he said into the phone.

His voice must have given him away. "What's happened?" Ash demanded. "Where are you?"

"Gare de Lyon."

"Gare d—! What's going on?"

"I'm on the run. Three men at least were waiting for me downstairs at Le Charlemagne this morning. I'm now wearing yellow hair, a torn T-shirt and a nose stud. But it won't be long before they're onto us again."

To give him his due, Ash took it all without protest, and went straight to the relevant word—"us."

"You're still with the woman you picked up in Verdun's office?"

"Ah…yeah. She's got green hair now."

"Isn't it obvious she's leading them to you?"

"Maybe. That's one reason to keep her close, though, isn't it? Find out what she knows."

"And if what she knows best is how to slip a stiletto between a man's ribs?" Ash demanded impatiently.

"I don't…" Haroun paused, his ears pricking, as two men speaking Arabic paused on the other side of the pillar. "I'll call you back, Ash," he said quickly in French, and disconnected.

He had recognized one of the voices. He couldn't put a name to it, but he was certain of having heard it before. Harry edged backwards around the pillar till he could hear their conversation. But he couldn't risk turning to look at them.

"Nice?" one of the men was saying. "Why should we go to Nice? Why do we leave Paris at all?"

"They were the only tickets I could get, and I had trouble enough getting them, too. From Nice we can get to Italy and catch a plane. The train leaves in an hour."

That was the voice he thought he knew. Not well. In the course of business, maybe.

"I think we should wait here in Paris for instructions," the first man said, in a mulish tone.

"There is more risk here than anywhere, Yusuf. If the Rose were taken from us now, what would your excuse be? Air travel was cancelled, the emissary did not arrive, and so we remained in a city full of spies and enemies?"

The hair on the back of Haroun's neck lifted with a kind of superstitious incredulity. Could he be mistaken? Hallucinating, even? No, he had heard it. *Al warda.* The Rose.

"Well, thank God that's done!" Emma exclaimed in her rich, warm voice which seemed so at odds with her new appearance. She was stuffing a wad of franc notes into the pocket of her jeans.

Fred reached for her and drew her close, stifling her surprised response with a finger on her lips. He leaned in against her neck like a lover.

"Careful! Do you see two men behind me?"

Mariel, her heart thumping, glanced over his shoulder. "Arabs," she murmured against his chest, while he bent his head to listen. "One short, thin, quite dark, about twenty-five, twenty-eight. Beard." Fred angled his body in against the pillar so that she could see the men past his arm. "The other—"

She paused when he touched her mouth. The other

two were speaking in Arabic. Fred listened, then, when the two fell silent again, prompted her to begin again. "The other?"

"Tall, lean, black beard. About thirty. He has a scar on his cheekbone, it pulls his eye down a b—"

She knew she had said something to electrify Fred. "Which eye?"

Mariel had a little trouble with right and left. "Right—no—yes, right side," she stammered. "They're going."

"Going!" He had to risk it. He couldn't lose this chance, even if it meant a deadly enemy would see and recognize him, too. Harry whirled, but too late. He got only a back view as the men moved into the seething crowd. Both wore casual pants and long-sleeved shirts. They carried one small red carryall between them.

"*Allah*, it's probably in that satchel!" he cried. "It was only inches from my hand!" He bent to snatch up their carrier bag.

"What—" Mariel began. Fred grabbed her arm, cutting her off.

"Come! We can't lose them! I need you to identify them for—"

Someone cannoned into her, blindsiding her, and Mariel smelled coffee and felt hot liquid streaming over her arm and breast.

She had time for no more than a choked scream before they were all over her. A dozen children, dirty and unkempt. One spread a torn copy of *Le Monde* in front of her face, and she could feel the little, questing hands everywhere on her body, patting pockets, slipping in and out, but she could neither get her bearings past the newspaper nor get her hands free. Coffee dripped down her arm.

She heard Fred cursing them and realized he was suffering the same fate. There was a babble of children's voices, and then they were simply gone, melting into the crowd in a dozen places.

"My money!" she cried, her hand going to her pocket. "They've taken all my money!"

"Mine, too," Fred told her. He held up the strap of his leather bag. It had been neatly cut. His T-shirt had a large wet patch, but at least when it dried it would be invisible. Her blouse was stained with coffee. "My phone, too."

"They even took the shopping bag!" Mariel wailed.

"Efficient little monsters," Fred remarked. He was patting his pockets. "Completely cleaned out."

"I'll have to phone my co—friend and ask him to wire more money immediately," was Mariel's first thought. It was the middle of the night now in California, but there was no help for that. "Oh, no!" she cried. "Do we even have change for the phone?"

Fred lifted his hands. "Not me."

"Oh, what a mess!" Mariel cried. "Maybe the police will let us phone. Where do we report it?"

"We don't have the time to waste on reporting it. Not the way we look now." Mariel bit her lip. It was true. Reporting to the police, especially dressed as they were, might merely be to waste hours, and to no benefit. Everyone knew about the children called "street Arabs," but no one ever caught them.

Mariel found she could almost laugh. "What on earth are we going to do?"

"One thing we are going to do, come hell or high water," Fred told her.

"What?"

He looked grim. "We are going to get on the Nice train that leaves in an hour."

"He pierced his nose and dyed his hair yellow?"

"Something to do with trying to evade the men on their trail," Ash said.

"Well, it worked with us and it worked for one other clumsy-footed set. Not sure about the others."

"He's got more than one tail, does he?" Ash observed dispassionately.

"Maybe as many as three. That's not counting us."

Ash swore.

"I'm completely snarled in traffic, the air strike is fouling everything. I've sent Charla by Metro—let's hope she gets there faster. Any idea why the Gare de Lyon? Know where he's headed?"

"He hung up in the middle of a conversation and didn't call back. When I tried his phone someone disconnected without answering."

"I'll let you know when I get there."

"Found something!" Mariel cried, stooping to pick up a coin. "Ten centimes!" she snorted. "Almost not worth picking up!" But she slipped it into her pocket, nevertheless.

They were wandering around the station looking for dropped coins, hoping to collect enough to buy a phone card. Without a phone card it would be a long and tedious wait before trying to arrange a collect call to Hal: the lineup for the single coin phone was ten times longer than for the banks of card phones. "I can't believe they got all your pocket change, too! Are you sure they didn't leave you even one ten-franc coin?"

"It was not the children who got my change. I gave that to a beggar before they dropped by," Fred informed her blandly.

Well, at least she was laughing. She shook her head. "You gave all your change to a beggar? Shouldn't that good deed have bought us a reprieve from those monster kids or something?"

"I don't think that's in the contract."

"It's not?" she enquired with mock ingenuousness. "There's nothing that says if you give to a beggar God guarantees you won't be robbed ten minutes later?"

"Recollect that the ways of Allah are mysterious. What looks like a tragedy to humans may be part of a larger purpose."

"Well, now that he's up in the world, maybe your beggar would give a little charity back." Mariel lifted her head and scanned the crowd. "You don't see him anywhere, by chance?"

Fred obediently lifted his head and threw a look around him. "Not in the immediate vicinity."

"Wait a minute! Beggar! What's he got that I don't have? I could beg!"

Fred looked at her. "Do you think so?"

"Yeah, why not?"

He shrugged. "You may not find it as easy as you think."

"You think there might be a territorial problem? Like those working girls last night?" She frowned, remembering how they had approached Fred, and how sharp the teeth of jealousy had been.

"That wasn't what I had in mind."

"Well, I'm going to try," Mariel said firmly.

She quickly learned what he meant. She found it much more difficult than she could have imagined to approach a stranger and ask for money. Especially as all around her tempers were so frayed. As the day progressed more people, including many families with small children, were packing into the station, and people did not seem to be feeling exactly charitable.

But it was an inner taboo that presented the biggest hurdle. It was bad enough being dressed as she was—plenty of people were looking at her as if she were of little worth already. Begging made her feel like nothing.

But recognizing an American accent, Mariel at last managed to make a firm appeal.

"I'll buy you a sandwich if you're hungry," the woman said when she had made her pitch, and Mariel wailed, "But I really do want to make a phone call!"

"Well, I won't give you money. I'm sorry. You look like you'll just go spend it on drugs."

She couldn't argue with that—when she caught sight of herself in a mirror she believed it herself. "But I won't! Look," she bargained, because now she had the bit between her teeth and was feeling a surge of energy, "would you buy me a phone card instead of food? Please?"

The woman pursed her mouth, considering. "Do you promise to use it and not sell it?"

"Yes! I promise!"

"All right. Where do you buy them?"

She came dancing back to Fred with the card held triumphantly high. They hurried to the phones. There was a lineup here, too.

As they joined the line, a sudden thought occurred to her. Mariel let out a horrified cry.

"What?" Fred asked.

"Hal's mobile number was in the pocket of my leather skirt! It's been stolen, too!"

Fred cracked up with a burst of laughter that she found totally infectious. "*Allah!* And mine were all in my phone."

Seven

"**Why** is it so important that you catch this train?" Mariel asked again.

"I have told you—because those two men are on it."

"That really explains a lot."

Fred heaved an exasperated breath. "And they have something that belongs to me and if I lose them now I lose my property forever."

"Oh." She blinked. "Is it valuable?"

"Immensely, to me and my family, and some others. Less so to the rest of the world."

"Well, if your friend doesn't get here soon, it's a lost cause."

Fred had phoned a friend whose number he had by heart. The friend had agreed to meet him at the station with some cash, but warned him that to get across Paris on this particular Saturday afternoon was not likely to take under an hour. That had been half an hour ago.

And the train was on the point of leaving. Because of the crowds, departure had been delayed, but it might go any minute.

Fred had dragged her down to the platform to watch those boarding so that she could identify the two men for him. She had watched the surging crowd avidly, but she had not seen them.

"What are you going to do if your friend doesn't come before the train leaves?"

"Get on it. You, too."

"Me?"

"If you do not see the men, you must come with me. I cannot explain now, but one day you will learn how important it is."

The fact was, it didn't really matter to Mariel where she went, as long as she was out of Paris. Nice was as good or as bad as anywhere else. She simply needed to kill time over the weekend until Hal got back into the office in California and she could call him on his office number. In a lot of ways getting by without money for two days would be easier out of Paris. And, of course, there was a part of her that wanted to stay with Fred, never mind where he went.

But still she kind of resented the suggestion she should be dragged along on Fred's enterprise, not for herself, but because she could identify the people he was really interested in.

So she said, "That's pretty high-handed."

"Shh!" Fred hissed a warning. "Look over there."

She looked, and saw surging humanity. "That dark man talking to the backpacker," he prompted.

She located them. An Arab with a wad of money in his hand talking urgently to a blond guy, probably an Aussie, who looked like one of the last few stragglers

for the Nice train. "He is trying to buy his ticket for
this train," Fred guessed. A moment later he was
proven right when the blond reached inside his jacket
and drew out a ticket.

Mariel shrugged. "We can't hope to do that without
cash."

Harry watched her closely. "He is one of the men
who followed us this morning at Le Charlemagne."

Mariel clutched at him. "Omigod, really? Are you
sure?"

He could not guess whether it was an act.

"Sure enough. Now look, we must not only get on
the train ourselves, we must at all costs prevent that man
from doing so. I have an idea."

"Excellency, forgive me, nothing can be attempted
here in the station. No escape would be possible even
from the concourse, and outside, the city is almost at a
standstill."

The speaker stood at a distance, alternately wiping
his brow and glancing over his shoulder to where his
partner was in negotiations with the backpacker in front
of the Nice platform. He could not be sure if the air
conditioning had broken down or if it was his own dis-
comfort making him hot.

"Zounab is attempting to buy tickets from those who
have already purchased them. It is the only way to ob-
tain a seat on the train, Excellency. It is obvious the
pair intend to board, they only wait for an accomplice,
perhaps." He bent his head and plugged one ear, listening.

"Excellency, if he is the one, we have nothing to
fear. A man with dyed hair and earrings—will such a
man be acceptable to the people? Let us follow him to

a less public place. If we were arrested, Excellency, our links with yourself could hardly remain undiscovered. Your cause would be done no service by such..."

His voice faded as a shout caught his attention, and he lifted his head again.

A man had collided with a stroller and was somersaulting over it in a display that had everyone staring openmouthed. It seemed he would end up winded or wounded on the ground, but he just kept rolling till he was on his feet again.

"Emma!" he cried. *"Non, ne me laisse pas!"* Don't leave me.

The agent on the phone recognized his quarry, and all his hackles rose. Tearing his eyes from the spectacle, he searched the crowd that had stopped to stare, and his heart sank.

Zounab was standing with his mouth open, staring at his empty hand. And the girl with green hair was running pell-mell towards the entrance to the Nice platform, the ticket firmly clutched in her hand.

"Laisse-moi seule!" she was screaming at the top of her voice. "I hate you! I never want to see you again!"

She waved the ticket at the astonished guard who, entranced by this scene of love gone wrong, only glanced at it. The girl broke into a run along the platform beside the train. Meanwhile the young man, with an agonized howl, called her name and gave chase. When he reached the guard he pushed past, crying, "Emmaaaaa! *Non!*"

He chased the green-haired girl down the platform along the length of the train and was lost to the speaker's view. Zounab belatedly gave chase but, having no ticket, was stopped by the guard. In the next moment the train's brakes were released, and it began to move.

The train was crammed to the rafters, with many people still standing in the aisles and vestibules, and luggage strewn everywhere.

Mariel, with Fred right behind her, slammed through the door, bounced off the opposite wall of the vestibule and, laughing in crazy glee, turned to watch him as his speed hurled him after her. He put out his arms to break his momentum, rolled against the wall beside her and ended up with his face inches from hers.

They lay there, laughing and panting, more from the risk than the exertion, as the train began to move.

"First stop Lyon," he declared triumphantly. One of her hair elastics had come off, and her soft green hair tumbled over his fingers. The pink stone in her nose stud winked at him. Her eyes darkened with a smile.

"That was quite a gymnastic display," she said. "I think you really must be a cat burglar."

Fred bent nearer and his other arm wrapped her waist as his mouth closed the gap between them.

What with breaking every rule in the book during the past half hour, Mariel's senses were pretty charged. The kiss put her over the top. A river of sunlight rushed through her blood, taking heat and sparkle to nourish every previously starved cell. She slid her arms around his neck and pressed against him. Shivery heat tingled her skin. His arm tightened around her back and she melted at the strength in it, letting him pull her over as he rolled with his back against the wall, his legs out to stabilize him, so that she was practically lying on him.

His hands ran down her back, pressing her, and then

wrapped around her waist again, as the kiss went on and on.

She lifted her lips, looking down at him, and soft delighted laughter escaped her. She could feel the pressure as his body stirred against hers, and immediately Fred smiled, straightened, and set her on her feet.

"More of that another time," he murmured. He took her hand and glanced around. There were several people in the vestibule with them, most of them looking at the couple.

Fred pulled open the door into the forward car. "We will walk through each car as if looking for seats," he murmured in her ear. "Look for the men you saw. If you see them, signal me." He settled his sunglasses on his nose, and immediately looked more dangerous. "Let's go. Walk slowly so that you can take a good look."

"Slowly" wasn't a problem. The aisles were full of people still stowing luggage and strollers, getting children settled with toys and games, looking for seats. This was not one of the new high speed trains; there was the relaxed feeling of people settling down for a long, familiar journey.

They quickly adopted the tactic of Fred looking on one side and Mariel the other. Whenever Fred spotted a man with a beard he would simply touch Mariel and she would glance over.

She was a little worried that she might not recognize men she had, after all, seen for only a minute or two, especially if they had separated. But when she finally did see them again, right at one end of a carriage by the luggage rack, rigid in seats that would not recline because they were against the wall, the recognition was unmistakable.

She touched Fred. "Last on the left," she murmured.

"Keep walking through to the next carriage," he commanded softly.

They paused by the two men for a moment waiting for the automatic door to open, then stepped into the vestibule. Mariel turned. "Did you—?" she began, but the rest of her question was choked off when she saw Fred's face.

Haroun felt as if he had been poleaxed. He leaned against the wall, sweat beading his forehead. *Ramiz.* He was much thinner, and the hair and the beard were a partial disguise, but Harry was in no doubt. He could hardly take it in. Ramiz Bahrami, a personal friend of Prince Karim of West Barakat. From a noble family who had always served the Barakati kings.

Almost instantly he remembered—Ramiz Bahrami was said to be missing. He had disappeared. It was said Prince Karim was distraught. Could that be disinformation? Was it possible that the princes of Barakat themselves were secretly supporting Ghasib against the al Jawadi?

God forbid. He would as soon believe that his own right hand had turned against him. Yet it was equally impossible to believe that Ramiz was betraying Prince Karim's interests.

Had he mistaken the conversation he heard? But the two men were sitting like guard dogs, the red carryall between them on the seat. If not the Rose, what were they guarding with such nervous ferocity?

"Fred, what is it? What's the matter?"

Allah, and he was weaponless. He was going to have to find a way to get hold of that carryall, and he had no tool but his mind.

"Fred!"

He blinked at her. "Emma," he murmured, like a man coming out of a trance. His hand clasped her upper arm, felt the warmth of her skin with deep appreciation. She could help. If only he could be sure of her.

"What's *wrong?* Are you sick? Is it your heart?"

"I'm fine." He shook his head. "Let's find seats, if we can."

He led her into the next car, his mind still whirling. Did the princes of Barakat want the Rose for their own purposes, perhaps? Could they mean to extract some concessions from Ash in exchange for it?

It seemed ridiculous; Ash was already committed to extremely favourable relations with the Barakat Emirates—how could it be otherwise? Such a course of action on the part of the princes could only damage their historically strong connections with the al Jawadis. Yet what other reason could they have for wanting the Rose?

The alternative was that Ramiz was an agent of Ghasib. They need look no further for their leak, if that was the case. It was almost unbelievable from the point of view of character, but at least it hung together circumstantially.

Ghasib was certainly desperate to have the Rose. With it, he could put forward a pretender to the al Jawadi throne and claim that he was the nominee of Sultan Hafzuddin. How could Ash prove otherwise? And a choice of candidates for a restored throne would inevitably undermine Ash's support.

That was all Ghasib needed. If Ash's base were eroded, the Islamic militants in Bagestan, always in the background and harshly repressed by Ghasib as a matter of deliberate policy, would undoubtedly make their own bid for power. Ghasib must be well aware that the vast

majority of the people did not want an Islamic regime.
They had been living in a secular state for over thirty
years, and the terrible spectre of Afghanistan's repres-
sive regime loomed large in everyone's imagination.
Women driven out of jobs, schools, hospitals. Left to
starve in the homes that they were forbidden to leave....

Faced with such a possibility, and with no certainty
that Ash could carry the day, waverers might well throw
their support behind Ghasib and his pretender. Better
the devil you know...

He had to prevent the Rose being delivered to Ghasib
at all costs. Thank God for the strike; otherwise it would
certainly be en route to Bagestan right now.

Most of the passengers had now settled into seats,
though some were up again, making the first foray into
the bar car or restaurant. The train had left Paris behind
and was making its way through countryside now. The
sun was bright on ripening fields.

In the next car they found two seats beside two Arab
women dressed in black chador. Fred asked in French
if the seats were taken and the women shrugged and
shook their heads.

"But we only have one ticket," Mariel reminded
him, in his ear, as they sat down facing each other.

"We must hope that the train is not completely full.
Some may have missed it because of the traffic," Fred
said with a fatalistic shrug.

All around them people were bringing out baskets
stuffed with bright tomatoes, bread, salami sausages,
cheese and butter, and settling down to a late picnic
lunch. There was beginning to be a festive air in the
train.

"Oh, I'm hungry!" Mariel exclaimed involuntarily,
eyeing the jovial family group across the aisle and get-

ting a waft of the delicious odour of fresh-baked baguette as *Maman* unwrapped two long golden sticks from a clean tea towel, broke one into pieces and passed them to two wide-eyed children. Papa, meanwhile, balanced a small cutting board on his lap and expertly sliced a white-powder-coated sausage with an ancient knife so often honed the blade was concave. "Do you think we picked up enough money to get a cup of coffee?"

Fred obligingly reached into his pocket, pulled out the few coins they had gathered, and turned them over on his open palm. Mariel could see at a glance there wasn't enough, and with a smile he replaced them in his pocket.

She realized with a sinking heart what a long journey it was going to be without food. It was ten or twelve hours to Nice on one of these slow trains. And her stomach was already saying that breakfast was ancient history.

She must have been unconsciously staring, because *Maman,* across the aisle, having carefully laid several slices of rich red tomato inside a buttered piece of baguette, handed it to one of the children with a low-voiced command, and the child turned to Mariel.

"Maman says would you like this?" the child said, holding the sandwich out to her.

Mariel was too hungry to pretend. "Yes, please!" she cried gratefully, taking the sandwich from the outstretched hand. "Thank you very much."

Maman and Papa and the little ones nodded gravely, and went back to business. Mariel, meanwhile, carefully tore her sandwich in two and passed half to Fred.

"Non, non!" cried Maman, who waved to show she was making another for Fred.

Next it was Papa's turn to offer the little board with the salami slices across the aisle, and in another few minutes there was a picnic atmosphere between the two groups. The Arab women brought out their own bag of food. They spoke little French, but they smiled and nodded and shared their food, too.

Between mouthfuls of the delicious supply of eatables Mariel told their story of the street children who had robbed them, exhibiting her coffee-stained blouse as evidence. "Only the tickets they missed!" she cried, cleverly pulling her ticket out of her pocket and waving it.

"And you got on the train with no money and no luggage! Where do you go? What will you do?" Maman and Papa cried.

"My brother's yacht is moored at Cannes," Fred supplied smoothly over Mariel's sudden stammer. "We are on our way to join him there."

Maman and Papa looked at Fred, subtracting the earrings and tattoos from his air of wealth and privilege, and believed him.

"Green hair?" Hal repeated.

"The only butterfly tattoo we could get a fix on at the Gare de Lyon was attached to a girl with green hair and a nose stud."

"Well, with Mariel it's always possible. If she had a good reason…where did she go?"

"She got on the train to Nice, chased by a man."

Hal sat up. "You got a description of the man?"

"Tanned, dyed yellow hair, tattoos, eyebrow ring. Screaming after her like an abandoned lover, people said. Quite a little show they put on."

"It can't be her," Hal muttered. "But still—"

"The agent I put on at Le Charlemagne says a hairdresser in the vicinity of Le Charlemagne reports dyeing a woman green this morning. And the man with her yellow."

"Can you get on that train?"

"We might take a helicopter to the first stop, Lyon, and try and pick it up there. Unfortunately, given the strike here, there may be no rental helicopters left."

"Buy one," said Hal.

When the meal was being packed away, Harry got up and wandered casually towards the front of the train. He came back after a few minutes, leaned down over Mariel as if looking out at the passing countryside and whispered in English, "The conductor is in the next car. Go into the toilet and stay there. Open the door when I give this knock."

He tapped her arm, long, short, long. Mariel blinked as the real world came back into focus. Her heart kicked, and she nodded, thanked everyone again for sharing their meal, then got up and made her way along the aisle.

Haroun casually sat down and turned to look out the window again, waiting until she had disappeared.

As another passenger came out, Mariel slipped inside the toilet and stood by the door, breathing slowly to calm herself. When she heard the triple tap on the door she opened it and stood behind the door as Fred entered.

She still wasn't quite sure how she had got into this situation, hiding out in a train toilet hoping to pull the old two-on-a-ticket routine.

"The conductor is just coming into the car. Give me the ticket," Fred commanded in a low tone.

She pulled it out of her pocket and handed it to him,

reflecting only after it was done that her first instinct seemed to be always to trust him. It was only when she thought about it that she had misgivings.

But that proved nothing.

It was an old train, and the cubicle had room for two. But it also had two mirrors opposite each other. If the conductor looked in he would see her reflection. "Can you crouch down between the sink and the door?" Fred suggested.

He turned on the hot tap and squirted a bunch of liquid soap into his hand. When the knock came on the door he touched her lips with a cautionary forefinger and opened the tap further, so the water gushed noisily out. The knock sounded again, keeping time with Mariel's thumping heart.

"Votre billet, s'il vous plait!"

Fred, rubbing the soap into suds, called something in Arabic. Then, in heavily accented French, *"Occupée, occupée!"*

"Bil-lets!" cried the conductor, banging the door.

At Fred's nod, Mariel crouched down behind the door. Fred, his hands and arms covered in suds, opened the door an inch and launched a volley of aggressive Arabic out the crack. Then, apparently realizing who it was, cried in fractured French, *"Ah, Monsieur, pardon. Billet, n'est pas!"*

Making as much of a business as could be out of it, dripping soapy water everywhere, he opened the door a few more inches. Mariel breathed out and made herself as small as possible as the door pressed against her.

Fred gingerly pulled the ticket out of his pocket and, still dripping, handed it to the conductor. In his clumsy attempts to avoid getting the man wet, he made things even worse, and then apologized in French so twisted Mariel had to bite her lip not to laugh.

"C'est le lave avant de prière." It is the wash before to prayer, he confided, in happy ignorance of the *contrôleur*'s contempt.

The conductor said something in rapid, colloquial French so insulting it was fortunate he wasn't looking into Fred's eyes, punched the ticket and handed it back. Fred thanked him with the broad smile and rapid nod of the besieged, willing-to-please foreigner, took the ticket and closed the door.

He handed Mariel the ticket. For a moment they exchanged a silent, conspiratorial smile. "Let's give it a few minutes," Fred whispered, went back to scrubbing his hands, and for good measure accompanied himself with a few loud bars of an Arabic song.

They had got over the first hurdle. But Mariel hadn't forgotten Fred's reaction when she had fingered the two men. There was more to come.

Eight

"I believe they are both on the train, Excellency."

"Does he have the Rose?"

"We think so. He was robbed at the station, but the Rose was not among the effects."

"Perhaps the thieves kept it."

"With respect, Excellency, no."

"Then get on the train and take the Rose from him."

"I have a helicopter waiting, Excellency. We shall catch the train at Lyon."

Mariel sat on the toilet as Fred dried his hands. "Do you think we're safe the rest of the way?"

Fred shook his head, turned and braced himself as the train went around a curve. "I have never been on this train before. It is possible they may check all tickets again after Lyon. But we must act before Lyon, in case they change their minds and disembark."

She didn't ask who. She knew that the two men and whatever they carried in their case hadn't been out of Fred's mind since the station. His eyes were clouded, as if half his mind was constantly worrying at the problem.

"Emma," he said now. "What were you doing in Michel Verdun's office last night? Who are you working for?"

It was the moment she was dreading. "I thought we agreed not to discuss things like that."

"It is not possible for me to go on in ignorance. Too much is at stake."

"There's a lot at stake for me, too," she pointed out.

He nodded, his eyes piercing her. "What, exactly?"

She wished they could confide in each other. She wanted to know that they were not working on opposite sides. But how would they ever get to that position?

"Tell me this," she said. "Is the thing you say those men have stolen by any chance a technological or industrial secret?"

"No." He shook his head, frowning, and propped his hips against the steel basin, his arms crossed. "No…is that what you're after? Industrial secrets?"

"Are you interested or involved in selling or passing on technology?"

"You are talking about theft?"

She simply looked at him.

"No," he said again. "I have absolutely no interest in industrial espionage. Neither the theft nor the sale of technology. Is Michel Verdun involved in such things as this, too?"

He sounded as though there was nothing he wouldn't believe about Michel Verdun, and Mariel laughed, feeling that it was safe to trust him a little further.

"I work for someone whose research and development work is routinely being stolen and sold on to foreign governments. We're trying to trace the source of the leak."

He nodded, hoping that was just what it sounded like—the simple truth. But there was a lot against it. "Why did you say, when you saw me in the office, *It's you?*"

Mariel bit her lip. "Because I had just been looking at a photograph of you that someone had e-mailed to Michel."

His eyes narrowed, and she suddenly felt frightened. "And did they name me?"

"I couldn't read the text message that was sent with it. It was in code."

He wished he could see into her heart.

"Now it's your turn."

Fred set his hands on either side of his hips against the washbasin and gazed down at her with an intensity that made her shiver.

"The two men you identified have in their satchel a ring that belongs to my family." She looked so disappointed he almost laughed. "But it also is much more than a jewel. It has an unimaginable symbolic value for many people. If these men are allowed to deliver it to the person who hired them to steal it, the ring, and a great deal more, may be lost forever. I have one chance now to get it back—to take it from these men before they get off the train. That means before Lyon, since I cannot be sure how long they will stay aboard. The lives and happiness of many people depend on me. I need your help to do it, Emma. Will you help me?"

Mariel was half hypnotized. "But...but how?"

"It will not be easy," Fred admitted. "It is a disadvantage to have no money. Another to be dressed so distinctively. But we have also one advantage—I know the name of one of the men.''

Mariel's eyes opened and she breathed an *oh*.

''Here is my idea. When the train is a few miles from Lyon, I will go to the luggage rack beside those men and begin to lift bags around as if I am searching for my own. You come up the aisle to where the men are seated, seem to recognize Ramiz suddenly, and call him by name. Ramiz Bahrami. He is the one with the scar. You start some kind of scene. Could you accuse him of abandoning you, or lying to you or something?''

''You mean, ask why he left me pregnant and alone?''

''You would not mind saying something like this in front of a carriage full of people?''

''You're talking to the girl here who dressed up as a lady of the night, remember?''

His eyes glinted and he lost his seriousness for a moment. ''Yes, I remember,'' was all he said, but with such a look Mariel lost all her breath.

She bent her head and stared at the stained grey linoleum beneath her feet. ''Yes, well, no, I don't mind, so what then?''

''Try to get Ramiz on his feet and away from the seats, leaving me to deal with his accomplice. *Insha'Allah,* I will be able to steal the bag and jump from the train as it approaches Lyon.''

''And then what?''

''The men are certain to follow me off the train at Lyon. You will simply stay on until Nice.'' She nodded. ''I will give you an address to go to where someone will help you. Will you do it, Emma?''

''All right,'' she said. There were a lot of potential

problems in his game plan, but she couldn't think of a better one. It was unlikely she would risk going to the address he gave her in Nice, though.

Maybe they would meet again somewhere.

As if reading her thoughts, he reached down and drew her to her feet. He put one hand under her chin. "We will meet again, Emma. We have unfinished business, have we not?"

Her heart kicked unmercifully, but she did her best to conceal it. "I don't know. Are you married?"

"Not married. My last girlfriend gave up on me because I travel too much."

"Then I guess we do have unfinished business."

"And you, Emma, are you married?"

"My last boyfriend didn't like me deciding to move back to France without warning."

"Ah, this is good." He smiled into her eyes. "And will you tell me your real name?"

She laughed. "Mariel. Yours?"

"What a delight to think that, no matter how easily others are fooled, we will never be able to fool each other. Haroun. Call me Harry."

"*Enchantée*, Harry."

He bent his head, wrapped her more securely in his arms, and gazed at her, only half smiling, as she lifted her lips for his kiss.

"Ah yes," he breathed, as his lips closed the little space. "Truly, I am enchanted," he murmured against her mouth, and then increased the pressure, sending rivulets of delight all the way to her toes.

After a moment, they drew apart. "Go out," he whispered, unlocking the door. "I will follow in a moment."

"*Bonjour, Mademoiselle,*" said the *contrôleur,*

who was waiting just outside. "And do you have a ticket, too?"

They were escorted from the train as soon as it stopped in Lyon, and taken into the station manager's office, where they were locked in. Haroun stood in frustrated fury in front of a window, looking out onto the platform with eagle eyes, watching the shift of the crowd.

"Reinforced glass," he muttered in disgust, flicking it with a knuckle. Mariel had an image of him hurling the desk through the window and trying to leap back onto the train, and bit her lip.

"At least we have a vantage point here," he said. "Ramiz and his partner have not disembarked."

He watched as two men tore through the entrance and leapt through the closing door of the train at the last moment. The train heaved a sigh and slowly pulled out of the station.

Harry sighed. "Now we have only to deal with this fool of a manager and catch up with the train at another stop."

Sitting by the window, Ramiz Bahrami absently watched the two men as they charged onto the platform and leapt aboard. He sat up abruptly.

"*Allah*, did you see them?"

"See who?" asked Yusuf.

"One of Ghasib's favourite hit men. Zounab al Safaak."

Yusuf stared. "On the train?"

"He has just boarded. With another." The two men looked at each other. "They are after us—what other answer is there?"

"But how do they know? How is it possible?" Yusuf stammered.

Ramiz leapt to his feet, grabbing the handle of the carryall. "We have been set up. A double agent somewhere. We've got to jump. Hurry, before the train gathers speed!"

Harry lifted his arm and pointed. "Here is a phone."

Mariel gratefully turned her steps towards the little café. The sun was low in the sky over the encircling mountains. The town, with its mixture of medieval and modern, was magical in the deep golden light.

Harry had managed to talk the station manager out of a determination to call the police. He had been convinced they were punk rockers making their way to next week's music concert in Fréjus, but Harry had pulled another tall tale out of his endless repertoire, to Mariel's secret admiration.

"Listen," Harry had said, leaning forward to pin the man with his eyes. "I see that you are a man for whom only the truth will do. I will tell you the truth, though it is a great secret. I am the grandson of the ex-Sultan of Bagestan. I travel in disguise, as you see. Two men on that train have stolen the al Jawadi Rose from us. It is of the utmost importance that we follow them. It is possible I am also being pursued by assassins. If you call the police, my mission will be lost...."

He was a mesmerizing speaker, and the station manager had not been proof against it, which Mariel could readily understand. It was an outrageous story, but she had half believed it herself. The manager, an Arab himself, had almost wept. He had actually bowed over Harry, and insisted on kissing his hand, and begged to be allowed to be of service. Mariel had almost given the game away by laughing.

The manager had been only too anxious to accept the reasoning that a single ticket to Nice covered two fares to Lyon, and therefore they had not robbed the SNCF of anything. He had even let Harry use the phone for a call to Paris. But there the luck had run out: no one had answered.

They were in for a run of bad luck, it seemed. They had caught a ride in Lyon with a man who said he was heading for Marseilles, but in the heavy, slow-going traffic south his car had begun to overheat almost immediately and he had pulled off the highway here, in the ancient town of Vienne. Harry and Mariel were now walking from café to café, looking for a phone that took phone cards instead of coins.

"I've never been to Vienne before," Mariel confided, stopping by a protective fence that surrounded an archaeological trench cut right down the middle of a side street. "When my school came on the trip I was sick, and I've never made it since." She gazed down into the deep hollow, but could see nothing. "I wonder what they'll find. Vienne has been settled since Roman times, you know."

Harry eyed the sun as he held the door of yet another café for her. "I think we will have to save the sightseeing for another visit. We have still to find a place to spend the night."

"Aren't we going to follow the train?"

"We cannot hope to catch up with it. There is no point now in going via Marseilles. The traffic will only get worse. We will do better on the country roads." His jaw was tight, but he didn't express his disappointment

in words. "We may as well head directly across to the
Côte d'Azur."

The café smelled of fresh bread and garlic frying in
butter. Mariel's stomach growled a demand and she
started salivating. A white-haired, very upright man
neatly dressed in a suit sat at a corner table, drinking
an aperitif. The waitress bustled around behind the
counter. She eyed them with dubious hostility, but at
Haroun's request, waved them to a phone on the other
side of the counter.

It was the type to take phone cards, and they heaved
a joint sigh of relief. Harry put the card in and dialled
while Mariel slipped off to the toilets.

Every time she caught sight of herself in a mirror,
she suffered a slight shock. She was always forgetting
what she now looked like. Well, it was an effective
disguise, if Michel was still looking for her. With a little
shudder she remembered the moment last night when
the taxi had passed her building and she had seen
Michel's car. That stopped her taking off the fake studs.
But she wished she could wash her stained blouse.

It did seem a horrible twist of fate that she looked
like this when she had met the man of her dreams. No
doubt they would part company before she got back to
normal, too. And when he thought of her, if he ever
did, he would have only Emma the hooker or Mariel
the grunge artist to remember.

"They got off the train? Where?"

The conductor frowned at the abrupt language. "I
believe the couple you describe were taken off at Lyon,
Monsieur, when it was discovered that they had only
one ticket between them, and no *cartes d'identité.*"

"My God, we came aboard at Lyon! We must have just missed them!"

"I am sorry, Monsieur," said the *contrôleur,* but his dry sarcasm was completely ignored.

"Where does the train stop next?"

"At Valence, Monsieur."

"Valence! It is too far!"

When she returned to the restaurant, Harry was talking on the phone in a low tone. "By what I overheard, Ramiz was planning to go all the way to Nice. But his partner was not happy about it. It'll be smart to get someone on the train at the earliest point, if the road traffic allows. The highway is practically at a standstill." He paused and listened. "Don't worry about me, put your efforts into getting onto Ramiz before he disappears. We'll make our own way. But get onto Ash immediately and tell him. My card's running out, but tell him I've got his number now and I'll call him when I can. All right, and I'll see you in Cannes."

"Let's have that coffee here," Mariel murmured, when he put the phone down. They had found another couple of coins in their wandering, and now had about enough change for one cup of coffee. She knew they should probably save it for later, but her stomach couldn't resist the delicious smells now wafting from the kitchen. She had to have something.

"All right," said Haroun, his eye going to the little blackboard with the chalked prices as he reached into his pocket for their collection of coins.

They were ten centimes short of the price listed for coffee, and Mariel let out an involuntary groan. "Oh, count it again!" she pleaded. She groped in her own pockets, uselessly, because she had given all the coins she found to Harry. Meanwhile, Harry, leaning on the counter, summoned the waitress with a beguilingly imperious hand.

"Monsieur?"

"I am sorry to trouble you, Madame, but we need your help. We have been robbed of everything," he told her. "We have picked up money from the streets, like beggars, and even now we are ten centimes short of the price of a cup of coffee. My friend is very hungry. Will you give us the charity of a cup of coffee at a reduced price?"

The waitress clicked her tongue. "Take that," she commanded, waving away the pathetic pile of coins, and as Mariel dejectedly turned towards the door, added, "Sit down." She nodded towards the tables. Then she set a tray and two cups on the counter, and picked up a two-cup *cafetière*.

They sat down. "Things happen around you, don't they?" Mariel told him softly.

Harry lifted his eyebrows and made no answer. The waitress approached with the tray bearing the coffee and a plate of half a dozen brandy snaps. They thanked her with undisguised relief and Mariel forgot what she was going to say and fell on the brandy snaps with a small moan, picking one up and tearing off its thin foil wrapping while she watched Harry pour the coffee.

He drank his coffee with appreciation, but when she pushed the plate of snaps at him he shook his head. "You eat them."

"But you're hungry, too!" Mariel protested.

"One of the advantages of fasting for thirty days each year is learning that one can do without food," he said. "I am used to it."

"But in Ramadan you only fast till sundown and then

you gorge," she protested. "This may be the last food we get today!"

He smiled. "No one gorges during Ramadan. We eat very sparsely."

"I thought there was a big feast at night," Mariel said, swiftly demolishing two more biscuits. Three were left.

"*Eid ul Fitr* comes at the end of the fasting month."

"Anyway, it's not Ramadan now, and you may as well eat your share," she said. But Harry only smiled.

"There is not enough there to feed a bird. You finish them," he urged, and she couldn't resist.

"Marthe." They turned at the sound of the call and saw the old man with his hand lifted. "These young people will be my guests for dinner," he said to the waitress. He nodded to Mariel and Haroun, and got to his feet. His hand invited them to join him at his table. "Please do an old man the honour."

"It is very kind of you, Monsieur," Harry replied, with an answering bow. "But I am afraid we disturb you."

"Not at all. I will enjoy the company. Allow me to introduce myself. I am Henri Saint Julien."

"Madame, as I have already explained to your colleagues, the girl with the butterfly tattoo and her partner were taken off the train at Lyon. If you doubt me—"

"You've already explained, Monsieur? Excuse me, but was someone else asking about them?"

"Not five minutes ago, Madame."

"And she got off the train at Lyon? Taken off, you say. Why?"

"She and her partner had only one ticket between them. They could not pay for another. And they had no identity cards on their persons. They said they had been robbed.'' He lifted his hands to show that he at least had not believed such a story.

"Robbed! Forgive me, Monsieur, but the girl is my sister. The family is very worried. She is with a man who—''

"I can tell you no more than this, Madame. I am desolated. But certainly the man is not one I would wish to find my own sister with.''

"And someone else was asking about them?''

"Two men, Madame. Dark complexioned. They showed more interest in the man. They were very disturbed to learn that the train will not stop again until Valen—good God, what is this happening?''

"It appears that the train is stopping, Monsieur, before Valence.''

"But this is outrageous! Someone has pulled the emergency cord! Where—excuse me, Madame, but I must—''

"But of course, Monsieur. I, too, have other business.''

Marthe brought their aperitifs, including a refill for the old man, and he lifted his glass to them.

"Now,'' he said when he had taken a healthy slug. "I ask you to tell me what it is like to be young today. I am very interested in the reasons behind the clothes and jewellery such young people as yourselves wear. Will you tell me why, for example, you have dyed your lovely hair such a colour, my dear?''

"For me it is only a disguise, Monsieur Saint Julien. The truth is, we are on the run from some very dangerous men,'' Mariel replied.

It seemed that the storytelling bug was catching.

Nine

"**I** will give you another example," Harry was saying half an hour later. "The swimming pools. The world knows that Bagestan is suffering the worst drought in many years. Children are dying. But who knows, or says, that this drought is the direct result of Ghasib's policies? To keep his international investors happy, to bring in the tourist money which goes straight into his own coffers, Ghasib continues to allow the swimming pools of the tourist hotels and resorts to be filled with fresh water. This drains the water table. And even today, in the middle of the drought, it still goes on. Children are dying so that tourists may have freshwater pools."

He had a rapt audience in Henri Saint Julien, Marthe the waitress, and Mariel herself, who was lost in admiration of his imagination. He had convinced them that he was part of a movement that was imminently going to oust the dictator Ghasib. The other tables in the restaurant were filling up, but Marthe was spending every spare minute in breathless amazement at theirs.

"I read something about that in the paper just yesterday!" she exclaimed. "One moment!" She excused herself to go and deliver plates of food to a neighbouring table. When she returned she held a tabloid newspaper.

"Look!" she said. *The Monster Who Starves His Own People,* read the garish headline. A smaller story was captioned *Where Is Our Sultan?*

"And this is you?" the old man queried, pointing to it. "Are you the man they are seeking?"

Harry lifted his hands. "Not me, Monsieur. *Insha'allah,* I will never be sultan. It is another who was named by my grandfather. I merely work to put him on the throne. Such a restricted life is not for me."

"No, of course not. Of course not," the old man agreed.

All too soon, the delicious meal was finished. "We must be on our way," Harry said, as they thanked Saint Julien again and got reluctantly to their feet.

"Thank you for telling me your stories," said Henri Saint Julien with another little bow. "I have enjoyed myself immensely. I wish you both all good luck, and I look forward to reading of your success in the newspapers. If you are ever back in this part of the world..."

Harry bowed his head once, looking regally gracious in spite of the eyebrow ring. "If we are successful in our bid, perhaps you will visit us one day in Bagestan and allow my family to return your very generous hospitality."

He turned to the waitress, who had been similarly entranced by his tales. "And you, Madame." He pocketed Monsieur Saint Julien's card, as well as one of the restaurant's on which Marthe had carefully written her name, and picked up the little carrier bag she had insisted on packing for them with a baguette and a half bottle of wine.

"Oh, how exciting it would be!" the waitress cried. "Good luck! Be sure that we will say nothing to anyone who asks about you!" She stood beside Monsieur Saint Julien as they left, waving as they turned for a last nod.

Henri Saint Julien seated himself again. Marthe turned to clear the table. "Will you have your coffee now?" She sighed hugely. "What a romantic story, Monsieur! How amazing that such a man should have come here, of all places! Do you think it will all happen as he hopes?"

"Yes, coffee, Marthe, if you please. We are certainly fools, you and I, but it was entertaining, was it not?"

"Why did you tell those nice people such wild stories?" Mariel asked, as they moved along the street.

"Why not?"

"You read that paper yesterday, didn't you?"

He glanced at her and did not reply. She was going to persist, but he looked at the sky and said, "The sun will set soon. We must think about where to spend the night."

"In the town?"

"It is dangerous to spend very long in one place. If we hitchhike into the country we may find somewhere more pleasant than a shop doorway. What do you think?"

Mariel thought she was enjoying hunger and homelessness in his company more than she had enjoyed feasting and luxury with other men, and smiled her willingness. Not that she was hungry now.

"Well, we've got the flask of wine and the loaf of bread," she said lightly. "So I guess we should find the wilderness. And the bough."

There was a steady stream of traffic, but no one seemed keen to pick them up. Eventually they caught a ride in the back of a pickup, where they shared space with some empty grape tubs and a black-and-white dog. The road wound through beautiful wooded hills and then opened out over a breathtaking valley. The air was fresh and invigorating, and the sun was kissing the tops of all the trees. There was a river sparkling along the valley floor.

Mariel leaned back against the cab of the truck with a sigh of contentment, and felt that life couldn't get more perfect than this. And then she was instantly proved wrong when Harry slipped his arm around her and drew her head to rest against his shoulder.

"This is a very beautiful part of the earth," Harry murmured, as peace enveloped them.

She had no idea how long they drove, into smaller and smaller roads, before the truck pulled up at the private drive to a vineyard. "I turn in here," said the driver. "If you continue down this road it will join a larger one that leads to Grenoble."

The shadows were very long now. On the right the land sloped sharply down to the valley floor. Here on the tiny back road there was little traffic. They walked on, not speaking much, listening to the evening bird-song. On a farm in the distance they heard the sound of machinery, a dog bark.

Mariel was thinking over the evening. She had heard Harry tell so many stories over the past twenty-four hours. He was a cat burglar, a rock music manager, on the trail of a stolen family heirloom, a sultan's grandson, and a man about to lead a revolution. She wondered if even he knew what the truth was. There were people who lived in a world of their own manufacture.

He seemed to have a charmed life with it all. In spite of having no money, they had eaten twice today. She was by no means the only person on the planet to find him utterly fascinating.

She had heard that con men were like that—so charming that their victims sometimes even refused to believe they had been scammed. And now she could understand that.

As for that wonderful apartment in the Rue de Rivoli—it would be nice to think that proved something, but Harry might have been running a con there, too. It was a pretty standard ploy for scam merchants; she had learned all about how people worked things like that from a prof who had made a study of it.

Harry had flicked her a glance now and then when he was telling his stories in the restaurant, as if trying to gauge their impact on her, too. That in itself was suspicious, wasn't it?

She knew she had to be careful, play safe, until she learned more about him. A lot more. She had to ignore the magic.

"Why that great sigh?" Harry asked with a smile.

She shook her head.

He noticed a narrow path through the trees. "Let's turn off here and find ourselves somewhere comfortable while there is still light to show us the way," he suggested, and with a nod she headed along the path. It was the first night she had ever spent homeless, but with Harry for company it seemed somehow normal and straightforward to be looking for a comfortable place to sleep al fresco. She looked up. The sky was clear and it promised to be a warm night.

He followed behind on the narrow trail, watching the sway of her low-slung hips. Now that he had passed over the pursuit of Ramiz Bahrami to others, he was free to concentrate on his own situation.

He wondered what the truth was. He could not dismiss the coincidence of her being in Verdun's office on the very night he broke in. And dressed the way she had been—Ash was right, of course. Ghasib was known to hire women assassins, and the possibility was high that she was one. How the bastard had figured out his, Harry's, psyche so accurately, picking a woman who appealed to him as if he'd designed her himself—well, he'd like to know the answer to that.

If she had had a knife in her boot last night it was possible she now had it strapped to one leg under the flares, but not very probable. He thought it more likely she had lost anything like that when the shopping bag went.

But nothing was certain, except that he wasn't going to part company with her until he knew more.

She was either the woman of his dreams or his worst nightmare. It wasn't a happy place to be.

"What are we doing here, Ramiz, in the middle of nowhere? What is your plan?" Yusuf protested.

Ramiz had drawn up at the crossroads, and was examining the map he had bought. "To avoid being assassinated by Ghasib, if at all possible. You do not share such an ambition?"

"But the Rose! How will we get to Barakat? What if we are attacked by thieves?"

"In the remote countryside that is much less likely

than in Paris. We will travel quietly along the back roads. It will take time, but it is better than letting Ghasib or al Jawadi agents have the Rose, is it not?''

''Al Jawadi agents? You think they are following us, too?''

''We can have picked up the Rose only minutes before their own agent arrived on the same mission. Of course they are looking for us. If they, too, think we are on the train, we may have already evaded them, but if they do not...''

''If they do not the answer is not to wander around this infidel country like two madmen, but to get to an airport as fast as possible and fly home!''

''If the strike is over by the time we reach Nice, everything is solved, isn't it?'' Ramiz retorted.

''Not if these killers are waiting for us there. We should hurry, not delay.''

Ramiz rattled the map irritably. ''You bleat like a thirsty goat! How can we hurry when every major road is at a standstill? I am doing what I can to be sure the Rose is delivered safely. Do you wish to take over the navigation of our enterprise?''

''I know nothing of France, but—''

''Then you had better leave it to me! Now, I suggest that we find a small hotel and order dinner there. If they are not already all full to bursting. In the morning we will think again.''

The river babbled a greeting as they sank down onto the soft grass of its bank. The sun was gone now, sunk behind the low mountains in streaks of brilliant red, and the valley was in the shadow of approaching night. A small animal scuffled in the undergrowth. The moon wasn't yet up, but through the trees the stars were beginning to show in a purple sky.

It was perfectly peaceful.

"This is wonderful!" Mariel flung herself back on the grass with a happy laugh. "Oh, that lovely old man! How kind of him to feed us that delicious meal, especially when you were stringing him such a ridiculous story! I'm sure he didn't believe a word of it."

Harry's smile glinted down at her. "You think I did not succeed in fooling them?"

"The waitress, maybe. But the old man *wanted* to believe you, I could see that! You really do have an effect on people, don't you?"

He stretched out on one elbow beside her and touched her cheek with a feather caress that trembled to her toes. "And you, Mariel—did you want to believe me? What effect do I have on you?"

She shivered, and her heart thumped. It was crazy to say that she was in love, but that was how she felt. The feeling she had had when she looked at his picture had only increased over the course of the last intense hours.

And she wanted nothing so much as to tell him. She wanted to reach her arms up around his neck and draw him down onto the grassy bed and whisper all her heart to him. Like an ache.

And no doubt that was the effect charming con men counted on, she reminded herself ruthlessly. She had to try to keep her head above water here, or she risked— she didn't know what.

So she smiled. "You're very sexy, Harry—" his lips came closer "—but it's only a few hours since I was calling you Fred. Who are you really?"

"Who do you think I am?" he countered, his fingers toying with her cheek and lips. Her hair was still caught in two bunches, making her look very young, and he lazily put out a hand to one and then the other, and pulled the elastics out, spreading her hair against the grass, green on green. He wondered why the sight was so erotic. Was there some primitive connection here in the fertile West between green and sex that he had unconsciously imbibed? She drew him as surely as if she clasped her hand in his gut and pulled.

"Who is the Green Woman?" he murmured, as the shadows darkened around them and the cicadas started their serenade.

Mariel smiled. "What?"

"The Green Man I know about—in some ways he matches our Khidr, the Guide. But who is the Green Woman?"

Now she laughed, her wide mouth mobile and made for kissing. "I don't really know. Some ancient fertility figure, I think. Celtic, maybe. She gives birth to trees or something, doesn't she?"

"Such fertile myths you have in the West," he complained. "Everybody is always giving birth." He stroked a lock of her hair and looked at the rushing river, which was black now as the light disappeared. "It is the water. Everything grows here, because you have water. Rain, and rivers, and lakes. Do you know why France was not conquered by the great Muslim army that conquered Spain?"

It was one of those conversations that is about anything except what it is about. His hand stroked her bare arm, she watched his mouth move hypnotically in the twilight, he saw the first stars reflected in her eyes. And they talked of other things.

"No, why?" she asked obligingly, struggling to subdue her skin's pleasure at his touch.

He stretched out an arm to the forest. "Because the commander of the Muslim army looked and saw the green of France. And he knew that his men would become soft if they inhabited such a land. So he turned back."

"And what about the Battle of Poitiers, when Charles Martel beat the Muslim army and killed their commander?" Mariel teased. "That didn't have anything to do with his decision?"

He laughed and waved a hand. "Ah, this was a different commander. But it is a truth, even if it is not a fact. Such a landscape as this changes a man."

He was distantly aware of meaning more than he said. He was talking about them, about her effect on him. When her eyes laughed into his it was like listening to the river. His heart lifted.

But he would be a fool to act on his feelings.

The darkness was almost complete. He sensed rather than saw her bend one knee up, reach a hand down to her calf. In the split second before he reacted, he smiled grimly to himself. A fool, indeed.

Mariel felt the questing insect crawl up her ankle and gingerly reached down to discourage it. If it was a carnivore or a stinger, she didn't want to do anything to startle it into biting.

A hand clamped her wrist with cruel precision, and suddenly Harry's body was half over hers, suffocating her. Her heart jerked under a surge of horrible, nauseating panic. She began to kick and struggle. What a fool she was! Why had she ever let her guard down? Why had she stayed with him when she had had so much opportunity to get away?

"No!" she cried desperately, but before she could

catch her breath to scream his other hand was firmly over her mouth.

She felt frozen in the moment. It was as if the world had stopped. She went passive for a second, and his hand released hers and began to slide around her calf under her jeans. Mariel's stomach heaved, and she twisted, trying to throw him off, smashing out at him with her fist.

How can this be happening, when I love him? her heart cried. She felt as though life itself had betrayed her. Everything she knew was turned on its head if he was capable of this.

Harry cursed and grabbed her flailing arm, and still she fought, kicking and panting. They writhed and grunted. At last he captured both her hands in one of his, his other hand over her mouth, his leg pinioning hers. "I will not hurt you, but I am going to disarm you, Mariel," he told her grimly. "If you do not struggle it will be over as soon as I have your knife."

He lifted his hand. She was panting in tortured moans, like a trapped wild animal, and he had to steel his heart against the instinct to release and comfort her. "Don't," she begged, as his hand again stroked her calf. "Please don't do this."

Harry frowned in the darkness. "I must have your weapon."

His words finally filtered through the terrible fear. "Weapon? Knife? What are you talking about?"

"You were reaching for it a moment ago, Mariel," he said dryly. "Now, let me take it. I will not harm you."

The tone of his voice reassured her a little, and insensibly her fear relaxed. "You think I have a knife?"

"Whatever you have strapped to your leg is what I want."

"Are you paranoid or something? Why would I be trying to kill you, Harry? Or is that just a handy excuse you give your conscience? Are you going to kill me?"

Meanwhile his hand was fairly methodically checking out her lower leg up to the knee, which was as far as the flares let him reach. He checked the other leg, then the grass beside her. After a beat, he released her.

Relief flooded her. She didn't know whether to laugh or cry or start shouting at him. They sat up, breathing heavily.

"I am sorry," he said. "You were reaching under the leg of your jeans."

"I was trying to stop an insect biting me!"

Harry gave vent to an incredulous snort. "An insect?"

Mariel pulled up the fabric over her calf and scratched indignantly. "The little wretch got me, thanks to you! I always go blotchy with bites, too. This will be the size of a two-franc piece by morning."

Harry fell on his back, laughing, and she glared reproachfully down. In the darkness his teeth were very white, and moonlight glimmered in his eyes. His laughter rang out through the trees, making some little forager in the undergrowth freeze in alarm.

"I thought you were trying to kill me, you thought I was attacking you, we have nearly destroyed each other—and all because of a mosquito? It's impossible!"

She clutched the remnants of her indignation to her. "I suppose I'll have to warn you every time I want to scratch," she complained, trying to resist the funny side, but with Harry cackling like a demon in the darkness that was impossible. "Harry, do you mind if I scratch?'' she mimicked, in a high, silly voice, and then in a deep one, ''Wait a moment, I will call my body-guards.''

He roared. She fell back against the grass beside him, exploding with laughter, and together they released the strain and horror of the past few ugly minutes and it floated away on their laughter. When it was over, they were left feeling a deep connection, and the curious, contradictory sensation that their suspicions had served to draw them closer.

The moon was coming up behind a distant mountain, turning the grass a deep purple-grey marked by the black shadows of the trees. The river's babble filled the silence. An owl hooted.

''Let's sleep now,'' he said. ''The sun will wake us early.''

Ten

Mariel awoke to find herself alone. Birds sang in the trees all around, and early sunlight spangled down through the branches. She sat up. Dew damped the grass, and she felt a little chilled.

Haroun was nowhere to be seen. He must have decided to go on without her. She supposed that was for the best, but the thought didn't stop her from feeling abandoned and alone. Mariel looked around, taking stock. He had left her the little bag of provisions Marthe had given them last night. She would eat, and then hitchhike into the nearest town. She would have to beg for the use of a phone and try to get in touch with her father. Her father would be able to arrange something.

If she could find him. She tried to remember their last conversation, and where he had said he would be for August. Well, she would call the house in the Dordogne, and if he wasn't there, someone would know where he was. Her father always seemed to have guests whether he was in residence or not.

If she'd called him yesterday she probably wouldn't be here now. Looking back now, she was amazed that she had actually got on the train with Harry. What had she been thinking of?

It had all happened too fast. Somehow, without realizing it, she had got into a way of thinking of them as a partnership. With her rational brain she had been telling herself it was possible Haroun was the enemy, but her feeling brain had decided otherwise.

It had been very chilling to discover that he was still so suspicious of her he thought she was waiting to slip a knife into him. She had had no idea that he still doubted her, though of course she had been harbouring suspicions about him, too.

With more cause, she reminded herself. She had heard him con nearly everyone he met. Why should he not be conning her, too? She was a fool if she thought otherwise.

She sat thinking over last night. The moment when he jumped her had been the worst moment of her life. In that moment she had understood that she had only been toying with suspicion. Deep in her heart she had believed that Harry and she were destined for each other. In the moment of seeming betrayal of that conviction her world had tottered.

It had been a far worse moment than the one when her parents had told her they were splitting. For nearly ten years that had reigned as her worst experience. But her parents were no longer the paramount figures in her life. They were not titans, just ordinary mortals trying to make life work, and not doing a very good job of it.

Funny, what love did for you. Who would have

guessed that falling in love with a total stranger would give her a more tolerant understanding of the bitter blow her parents had dealt her?

You're crazy, part of her whispered. *You can't be in love, you don't know him!*

But she did know him. The heart does not need a lifetime.

And he had left her and she had no way of tracing him. Unless he wanted her to find him. Maybe he would. The best thing she could do now was get on the road. With luck she might catch him....

Absently Mariel dragged open the bag of provisions, then stopped. Her blouse was stained with grass as well as coffee now. Her hands were grubby. She needed to wash. She kicked off her shoes and dragged off her jeans and went down to the river, but just here the stream was running fast over stones. Mariel turned and headed upriver, looking for still water.

She found some just around a bend. Harry had found it before her, and was still in it. In a purely instinctive reaction she dodged behind a bush.

She was aware of a huge sense of relief. Clearly he had no intention of abandoning her. Perversely she wondered if she should use this chance to abandon him. If she caught a ride quickly, which was just possible on a Sunday morning in the country...

He was naked in a shallow pool of water formed by a bulge in the opposite bank. The sun glistened on his skin and his crazy, bright yellow hair. He was scrubbing himself with handfuls of sand from the river floor, paying particular attention to his fake tattoos.

She forgot to think and began to be entranced, slipping into a strange, timeless world. He was completely and utterly gorgeous. Supple, slender, muscled, beautifully proportioned, with not a spare ounce of fat. He had a gymnast's body. No wonder he could do such things as that rolling somersault over the child's stroller he had executed in the Gare de Lyon.

His skin was the same warm shade all over, with a black mat of hair on his chest trailing in a line down to the one on his groin. His stomach was flat, his haunches lean.

He finished his scrub and moved over into the deeper, flowing water and sank underneath. The undercurrent caught him, so that he was dragged downriver a little towards her, and when he came up, blowing, he suddenly seemed not to be able to find his footing. He choked out a cry, made a grab for the bank and missed, and then was caught in an eddy and dragged helplessly along.

"Au secours!" he cried, as his head was dragged under again.

Mariel thanked God she was already stripped down to blouse and briefs, and ran to leap in. But he was suddenly carried closer to the bank, so instead she flung herself flat at the edge, leaned her upper body out and reached for him.

"Harry!" she screamed as his head came out of the water.

He saw her, and with a cry he reached up and his hand met hers and clung. With her other hand she clutched the long grass at the water's edge and tried to pull him towards her, but she could feel his cold, wet hand slipping from her grasp. He lifted his other hand and took a firmer grip, but now the drag was too much. She was being twisted around so that her grip on the grass was useless as support. She was pulled further over the edge and began to overbalance.

"Let go and I'll try again further down!" she panted, but his hands were locked to hers now and he was kicking frantically, seeking purchase on the bottom.

"Too deep!" he moaned, and then the inevitable happened: he spun around in a little eddy, and Mariel was dragged off balance completely and with a cry tumbled down into the water near him.

It was a mountain stream and it was cold. She shot to the surface and gasped for air. Harry reached for her, and she felt his arms go tightly around her and thought with curious calm, *If he panics we'll both drown.*

And then he wrapped her in both arms, pressing her to him, and his teeth appeared in a wide smile and he was *laughing!*

She could hardly believe it. The shift was too sudden.

"What's happening?" And then, in a different voice, "What do you think you're doing?" she demanded, her fear dissolving into righteous anger as her brain worked it out.

"What were you doing there, spying on me?" he riposted, still laughing. "Have you never seen a man before, that you hide in the bushes to watch?"

She discovered that there was no answer she could make to this. She felt like a complete idiot. She drew out of his dangerously enticing hold, dog-paddling against the slight current.

"I wasn't really spying. I was surprised to see you. I thought you'd gone."

Harry was still grinning. "So you were looking to make sure it was me? And how did you recognize me?"

He was actually standing on the bottom—the water was scarcely five feet deep. "Never mind," Mariel said. She swam to the bank and heaved herself out. She had

had enough of a bath. She certainly wasn't going to scrub herself with sand in a freezing cold river.

Her soaked blouse and briefs clung to her, and to hell with him. Mariel stood with legs astride, bending over to wring out her hair. After a pregnant pause, she heard Harry get out some way along and walk up to where he had left his clothes.

It was only then that she realized she had been holding her breath. What had she expected him to do? Make love to her?

She made her way back to where she had left the bag of provisions. There she slipped off her wet blouse and briefs, dried herself down a little with her jeans, then put them on. She rinsed out her briefs and muddy blouse in the stream and spread them to dry on a bush in the sun. Harry was so cool, she was quite sure he could handle toplessness, and if he couldn't...

"Shall we have breakfast?" Harry asked, behind her. "I think you should take this."

She turned, instinctively covering her breasts with one arm, and his loins leapt. The small, full breasts, long, curving waist, smooth abdomen, round hips all seemed to have been made for love. Made for him to love. The little butterfly tattoo fluttered with her shallow, startled breathing. Two birds ruffled and twittered on the branches above him, as if to urge him on.

Harry was naked to his waist, and holding out the black T-shirt. She seemed to feel heat emanating from his body, warming her at a distance of four feet, and making her want to slip up against that warmth and have his arms around her.

"Thank you," she said, not protesting, because even a low-key argument would lead in unpredictable directions. She pulled the damp T-shirt over her head and they sat down to their breakfast, courtesy of Marthe. As well as the baguette, she had put in a chunk of cheese, a salami sausage, two tomatoes and even a knife.

Mariel's stomach gurgled in happy anticipation. "You really must reward her when you get back into your palace in Bagestan!" she joked.

Harry was slicing the tomato. He glanced at her. "But of course," he said.

There was something about the way he said it. Mariel frowned, for the first time wondering if the nonsense she had heard him spouting yesterday might have a grain of truth.

"Harry..." she began tentatively. Then common sense took over, and she laughed. "Nothing," she said, taking the slice of tomato he offered.

"I picked up the trail in Vienne this morning. They're still together, apparently. He's now claiming to be some kind of sultan in disguise."

"Great!" Hal groaned.

"They still have no money. They seem to be heading down to Fréjus, though, so I imagine our first source was right and they're heading for the music festival there."

"Mariel's always been a bit unpredictable," Hal murmured. "I don't know about that, though. I had someone question people who got off the train at Nice, and a woman reported that the man said his brother had a yacht at Cannes."

"He's a real con man, no doubt about it. The waitress I questioned was heartbroken when I said my sister was being shanghaied by a crook. She believed every word he said."

"It's crazy."

"Hal, he may be drugging her."

He cursed. "Right, I didn't think of that. Well, it makes sense of the green hair, I guess."

"Thank God she did it. Makes my job easier—people remember when a girl with green hair and a butterfly tattoo has been by."

"What are you going to do now?"

"Something tells me they won't get very far on a Sunday even on the back roads. Stands to reason anyone who picks them up won't be going far. Church and back, or *Grandmère*'s for Sunday lunch. So I think the best thing I can do is sniff around here a little longer, see if I can pick up the trail. If they *are* headed to Fréjus they'll probably stay there for a few days, anyway. The festival lasts five days, I think. I can catch up with them there."

"What's *that?*" Mariel cried in amazement. "The Beatles bus?"

They had been walking for nearly two hours. Today it had been even harder than yesterday to get a ride, perhaps because, deep in the countryside, people were more suspicious of them. Or because Harry wasn't wearing a shirt. Or because many of the cars were filled with family members. But they didn't stop trying. They put out their thumbs with each new appearance of a vehicle.

The bus was coming around a bend about a hundred yards away. An ancient bus with an old-fashioned, prominent nose, wheezing and creaking, and painted every colour in the spectrum in a pattern of wild swirls and blossoms.

"I've never seen a bus like that in real life before!"
she laughed.

"I have seen things like this in India," said Haroun.
"Perhaps that is what they took their inspiration from."

They stuck out their thumbs and the old bus coughed
to a standstill. Along its side, in a swirling logo that
matched the intricate paint job, she read, *The Travelling
Circus*. The doors strained, protested and then suddenly
banged open.

"Hello," cried a young voice in English. "Heading
to Fréjus?"

"Yes," Harry said instantly.

"Climb aboard, then."

They went up the steps and inside, and stood blinking
in surprise. "Hi!" cried a chorus of voices, and they
found they had stepped backstage at a theatre.

The bus had been stripped of its ordinary seating and
turned into a large camper van, with a kitchen, dining,
and sitting area. There were about a dozen passengers,
all young.

At the far end, sitting on a sofa that ran around the
sides and back of the bus, a girl in a minuscule sequined
bikini was putting on makeup. It was a space that
clearly doubled as sleeping quarters. Above the seats a
low ceiling created additional bunk space.

Other people in various states of undress were bent
over some trunks that sat against one wall of the bus,
or fiddled with various kinds of equipment. They all
looked under twenty. Most of them seemed to be smoking, but at least the windows were wide open.

"Anybody object if I'm the wizard again?" someone
called.

"Not so much of the pink smoke this time, then,"
another voice cried.

The small galley was behind the driver, who was dressed in a leopard skin and little else.

"I'm Mike," he said.

"Hi, I'm Mariel."

"Harry," said Harry.

"Grab a seat, mate."

The bus started again as they moved inside. Midway along the bus a thin boy with blue hair was standing at an ironing board, working the iron over something composed of dozens of brightly coloured petals.

"I must say, Jerry as good as ruined this parrot!" he cried. Then, as they approached, "Hi, I'm Brian," he said. "You're heading for Fréjus, too?"

"Down to the coast, anyway. Is that where you're headed?"

"Yeah, Fréjus is our last stop. The festival. Then we go home."

"Will you stop fussing with that thing, Brian? I need the iron," a girl lounging nearby interrupted impatiently. She had an Australian accent.

"It got very crushed, the way Jerry folded it," Brian retorted defensively. "I don't want all my feathers turning up at the end, do I? Looks seedy. Kids don't like it."

He held up the object, twitching at the petals, and now they could see that it was a costume of some kind. It had short legs and big flapping arms and an orange, red and yellow tail.

"I'm Angela, by the way," the Australian girl continued. "I hope you two have a taste for performance art."

Mariel laughed. "You really are a circus?"

Several of the others had moved towards them. "How far now, Mike?" one cried.

"About fifteen minutes."

"Hell, I've got to get going!" a girl cried.

"Be all right if Brian would get off the iron," said Angela.

"All right, all right, you can have it, but don't blame me if people complain we look tacky."

"You watch how it works this time, then at the next stop maybe you'll join in. We're a bit short-staffed—a few have left the project early. Right now you'd better get out of the way, just sit over there," Angela urged them.

They obediently moved down to the end of the bus, where the girl with the makeup proved to be gluing sequins all around her eyes.

"This was our gap year project," she explained when they got talking. "We all did drama for A levels. Jordan and Annie come from Canada—they were at a high school for the performing arts, weren't you, Annie?" she called, and a girl in all-over brown Lycra with a long velvet tail came to sit down.

"Yeah, in Toronto. I've got a place at the National Theatre School in Montreal starting in the fall. You're American, aren't you?" she said to Mariel. She was carrying a large monkey-head mask and a brush, and began grooming the mask's fur and whiskers.

"Half French, half American," said Mariel.

"And what are you?" Annie tilted her head towards Harry with a provocative smile.

"Half Barakati, half Bagestani. And now, with French citizenship," he replied, and even with that simple, straightforward comment, Annie visibly melted under his charm. Her eyes ran hungrily over his naked chest, and Mariel was really sorry suddenly that she hadn't put on her wet blouse instead of Harry's T-shirt.

"Oh wow, Barakat! Did you ever meet those princes?"

"But of course. I am Cup Companion to Prince Omar."

Everybody laughed.

"Cup Companion! Oh, I've heard about them! They're always in the magazines. Boy, I'd love to meet one!"

"They're all so gorgeous, those guys!" Angela sauntered up, wearing a sexy black panther costume. She grabbed a railing for support, bent to catch one ankle and began to stretch her leg up to her head, steadying herself against the sudden sway as the bus went around a bend. It looked casual, no doubt her usual warmup, but Mariel knew who it was directed at. "You could almost be one, except for the hair."

"You think I should change my hair colour?"

"I've always wondered what it means, actually, Cup Companion," someone said. "What do they do?"

"Many different things. Some oversee various areas such as trade, or tourism, providing non-partisan support for the country's exporters, for example," Harry told them, with such unconscious authority in his voice that they began to throw him speculative looks.

"What's the Cup stand for?" someone asked.

"The traditional role was very different. In ancient times, the cup referred to was the winecup. Cup Companions were the men with whom the king relaxed and enjoyed himself. They never discussed the country's affairs with him, but only matters of pleasure, such as poetry, philosophy and music. Modern Cup Companions, however, are the monarch's eyes and ears in the country. They are like a cabinet."

"Okay, we're there!" Mike cried. "Menagerie to the front, please!"

The bus drew up in a sun-filled village square, and Mike pulled the handle to open the door. There were a few people standing in the square talking; others were coming out of the steepled stone church. A couple of children were already chasing over to the brightly coloured bus as Tarzan leapt down the steps, accompanied by a monkey and a cat who cartwheeled over the cobblestones.

The babe in the sequined bikini followed, tossing juggling batons into the air as she went. Then a clown carried a tape deck playing cheerful music, and the parrot followed him. By the time the whole circus was out of the bus, quite a little crowd was gathering in the square. Mariel and Harry followed to watch.

They performed in turns, Tarzan, the monkey and the black panther starting things off with an impressive display of leaps and flips. After a few minutes the monkey took off her red fez and with cute mimes canvassed the watchers for coins before backing away to let the juggler do a stint. Then the juggler, too, pulled off her sequined cap and begged. The wizard walked around making things appear from behind children's ears, and handing out leaflets to the adults.

Mariel took a leaflet herself. In Canadian French, it explained that the group were students engaged in a drama project and needed donations to carry on.

Within half an hour the circus was taking the final round of applause. Then everyone leapt back into the bus and, the children waving goodbye, they drove off.

"We've been doing it for a year now," Annie explained. "Well, most of us have. A few people have left and others have joined. We got startup money to set us up with costumes and the bus, but we support ourselves performing. We've been all over England and Europe. It's been a fantastic year!''

''Apart from sometimes having to run from the *flics*,'' Jordan chimed in. ''We ought to ask permission from the local cops at every stop, but that would take forever. That's why we avoid the bigger towns. Out here usually they don't bother to notice us, and when they do they never do more than chase us off. But in the big towns it's different.''

''It'll take us a couple of days to get to Fréjus,'' Brian the parrot said. ''We've got room if you want to stick around.''

''The thing is,'' Angela said, ''if you do want to come along, you'll have to contribute to the food and petrol. We don't earn much more than our keep.''

''We have traced them to a few miles beyond Vienne, tell his Excellency. There the trail runs cold. A few people saw them on the road this morning, but no one picked them up. It is possible they know we are on their trail and have taken refuge in a barn or something. Or perhaps they are walking across the fields. But we will pick up the scent again.''

Mariel was given a skimpy costume, net stockings and a cap with a feather, all in shades of green, to which her hair added another note, and was informed she was Maid Marian for the rest of the day. She made her entrance butt first, slung over the shoulder of Mark, the Sheriff of Nottingham. Harry was Robin Hood, and rescued her from the sheriff. The two men ran through the crowd shooting imaginary arrows at each other, one executing a dramatic roll or flip whenever the other got a bead on him, while Marian swooned attractively and then pulled off her cap and collected from the crowd.

"The thing is, the Papas like a little sex, and they're the ones with the pocket change," Angela explained unnecessarily as they moved between stops. "That's why the babes do most of the collecting. And the wives don't mind because it's innocent fun. Papa can ogle the legs all he wants, she knows it's not going anywhere. So it's usually okay to play up a little. Actually, you're doing well." She eyed Harry appreciatively. "We haven't done Robin Hood for a while. I forgot how much they like it."

They did so well, in fact, that when they stopped in a larger town, where a *pharmacie* was open, Mariel was able to go in and buy two packets of hair dye. *Nuit* for Harry was easy, but she wondered if the *marron glacé* she bought for herself would really restore her original colour.

At nightfall, the bus stopped by another little river, and they built a fire and cooked and ate a companionable meal. Afterwards, in twos and threes, the company went down to the river to bathe.

Mariel produced the packets of dye, tossing one to Harry where he still sat by the fire, talking to Brian and Angela. He caught it and flicked her a look that melted her where she stood. She told herself sternly that he meant nothing by it. She was no different than Angela, aroused to sexual display by his mere presence.

"What does this mean?" he asked, with typical male ignorance. "We do this ourselves? Don't we have to go to a specialist?"

Brian blinked at him. "What—didn't you do that yellow job yourself? I never go to a hairdresser."

"I have much to learn," Harry said, mock submissive. He got to his feet. "But Mariel will teach me all I need to know."

He guessed how she felt and was playing with her, she was sure. Well, it wasn't much of a guess—every woman she'd seen had been entranced by him. He must consider it a fact of nature, like gravity.

Or electromagnetism.

So she massaged the black colour into his hair, wrapped it and told him severely to leave it alone, then did the same for herself. When it came time to rinse, she made him kneel with his head over a bucket and poured water over his head. They poured the dirty water over a stony patch of ground, so that the dye would filter through the earth rather than go straight into the river.

She ran the fingers of one hand through his hair as she rinsed it, feeling how deliciously silky it was, and revelling in the sense of intimacy that crept over them as they worked. When he was thoroughly rinsed, Harry performed the same service for her, fetching buckets of water from the river and pouring them over her head as she knelt on the grass.

By the time they returned to the campsite, most of the company was bedding down. Mariel knelt by the dying fire to dry her hair. She realized with a slight shock that tomorrow was Monday. She could get Hal's business number from long distance information and phone him after nine o'clock in the morning California time. That wasn't till 6:00 p.m. French time, but it meant her troubles would soon be over.

If she called them troubles...

"Oh, Harry, you look much more like a Cup Companion now," a girl laughed as he sank down in firelight. "Listen, everyone, we haven't done the *Thousand*

and One Nights thing since Greg left! Why don't we do it tomorrow? Harry can be the sultan!''

All around the campfire, voices were raised in lazy agreement. There was space wide enough for two bodies in the neat circle of sleepers, with a couple of folded blankets lying in obvious invitation.

As she wrapped herself in a blanket and settled down too close to Harry for comfort, Mariel felt his suppressed laughter, but was too tired to wonder for long.

Eleven

***

"**O**h, wow, you sure do look like a sultan now!"

Harry glanced from his admiring audience to look down at his shimmering gold lamé trousers. They sat on his hips under a wide, pointed, embossed gold-and-black belt, and were baggy and drawn in at the ankles. On his feet were gold shoes with turned-up toes.

"No self-respecting sultan would allow himself to be dressed in such clothing as this. It is more suited to a genie from a fairy tale," he told them emphatically, shrugging into the silky black robe with its intricate patterning of gold appliqué.

"Genie or sultan, you get my vote," Angela told him.

He really was heart-stoppingly handsome. The change back to black hair underlined his dark attraction, and all the girls stood around him in their harem gear, smiling involuntarily. The men were perhaps a little less pleased.

"And now the djellaba," Angela cried, handing him a length of gold lamé cloth and a circlet of black rope. "Am I pronouncing it right?"

"What—with *shalwar* such as these?" Harry shook his head emphatically. "No."

"Jill-aba?" Angela queried.

"What?—oh, you pronounce it fine, but I cannot wear it. The heart revolts."

"I thought Arabs wore..."

"Give me the fez that the monkey wears," Harry commanded, tossing the black rope to one side. It was passed to him instantly, a fact he scarcely noticed, but Mariel did. Harry set the fez on the back of his head, picked up the length of gold cloth, and began to twist and wrap it expertly around the fez. When he came to the end, he tucked it in some mysterious way. He turned to them. His hair curling out under the small, neat turban, his eyes glinting, he looked like a picture from some long-ago book of tales.

"Sultans in fairy tales wear turbans," he announced.

"Oh God, you look just like a sultan, Harry, you really do!"

"We should have had you all year!"

"You need some jewellery, don't you?" Angela suggested, bringing him the big jewel case.

Mariel, meanwhile, was dressed in an equally fantastic harem costume. It was made of fine white muslin, a pair of low-slung harem pants and a top that only covered her breasts, leaving the long expanse of her midriff and abdomen bare. Around the breasts, the short sleeves of the top, across the hips and at the ankles, the cloth was stitched with gold embroidery and studded with fake rubies, emeralds and sapphires.

The legs of the pants were slit down the front from mid-thigh to the ankles, seductively revealing her legs as she moved. There was a gathered half-skirt attached behind, ankle-length, lined in gold.

There was also a waist-length black curling wig with little kiss-curls around her temples and cheeks, a gold coin belt to sling around her hips, a circlet for her fore-head, as well as bracelets, necklaces, rings and scarves.

And two little pairs of cymbals, sign of the belly dancer's art.

Mariel picked them up now, slipped them on her fingers, lifted her arms and made them clatter.

"Oh, you know how to do it!" Annie exclaimed.

Mariel laughed. "I used to take belly dancing classes. It's terrific exercise."

"Oh, so you can really do the dance?" Angela said, trying to inject enthusiasm into her tone. "That's great, I wish I could."

"Why have we not reached the Mediterranean, Ramiz? Surely France is not so big as this!"

"I am sure it is very close. Perhaps I made a wrong turn."

"Again?"

"It is difficult in these mountains."

"We're working our way up from Cannes, Ash, and there hasn't been a sign of either him or the girl. We're working the other side of Vienne and it's the same story there. They were seen travelling out of Vienne, going vaguely southeast, on Saturday evening. Sunday morning they were walking on the same road. Nothing since then.''

Ash was quiet for a long moment.

''Ash, there are one helluva lot of villages in this part of France, and many ways they could have gone, including off the road. Somebody mentioned a travelling circus being in the neighbourhood. We're going to check that out. Always a possibility.''

''Yeah,'' Ash said, unconvinced. ''Well, keep at it.''

''Hal! Pay dirt! A girl with green hair bought two packages of hair dye here yesterday afternoon! The woman thought they were with a bunch of Gypsies taking a rainbow-painted bus down towards Fréjus! She says they've been stopping every few villages to beg. I can't be far behind them at that rate.''

''Terrific,'' said Hal.

''Sorry to wake you in the middle of the night, but you did say call as soon as I had a lead.''

''For sure.''

''Well, that does it! I'm going to take up belly dancing as soon as we get back home!'' Annie declared, as they lounged in the bus counting the take that afternoon after their third stop. The crowd had been more than usually generous again. ''And on a Monday, too!''

The *Thousand and One Nights* was a hit, a very palpable hit. When they tumbled out of the bus in front of the bemused eyes of shoppers, shopkeepers, businessmen, tradesmen, children and mothers with babies all going on their workaday round, they created a sultan's harem, and everyone apparently loved it.

''It's because Harry makes such a spectacular sultan,'' Angela insisted, and it was certainly true that, as well as being handsome as the night in his black-and-gold costume, he had an air of command that was deeply compelling.

"Be fair," said Annie. "It's also Mariel's dancing."

"This looks promising," said Brian, who was driving, as they neared the centre of a small town. At the centre of a crossroads between two stretches of shops and businesses was a circular, grassy park, with a few flowerbeds, raised from the ground and shored by neat brick. "The town's a bit bigger than usual, though, chaps, what do you say? Want to risk the *flics?*"

For some reason they were all a little punch drunk. "Sure!" "Great spot!" everyone agreed, and Brian pulled up and parked.

The troupe spilled off the bus again, dancing and cartwheeling over the road to the little parklet. In the middle of them all was Harry, sitting regally cross-legged on a large cushion borne by four male slaves, all barefoot and naked to the waist in white *shalwar* and djellabas. He was set down in the centre of the circle of grass, with a hookah on the ground in front of him. The others cavorting around were all there to entertain him: the monkeys, the juggler, the magician, the gymnasts, the slaves. And the belly dancer.

The tape deck was blasting out Middle Eastern music as, one group at a time, summoned by an imperious gesture, they showed the sultan their tricks, then bowed and held out their caps to him. The sultan would start the ball rolling by grandly tossing each a huge jewel. Then they turned to the crowd for further donations.

The sultan lazily beckoned the belly dancer, his rings glinting in the afternoon sun. At their previous stops they had discovered that she was a crowd pleaser. Mariel announced her presence with the belly dancer's piercing *lalalalalala* as she ran to a spot before the sultan in a whirl of scarves and, by way of introduction, began to spin in place, her bare feet neatly circling, hair, scarves and skirt flowing out around her, hands up and fingers clicking.

That got their attention.

Then her hips started to move with the music. Her skirt flowed hypnotically, and the flash of skin as her knees appeared and disappeared in the fabric's soft folds captured the attention of more men than the sultan.

Mariel had never before done the dance anywhere except the exercise studio, and she had never danced in front of men. Nor had she worn such a sexy costume before. But most of all, she had never before today had the eyes of the sexiest sultan in the world on her, glinting with erotic approval.

Up and down the streets that led to the green, people had been slowing their pace, turning their steps towards the sultan's playground, as the wild Eastern music charmed the air. More dangerously, the cars coming into the roundabout slowed as drivers stared at the spectacle.

It was a bit like being drunk. Mariel smiled, her hips swayed, and all the steps she had so painstakingly learned suddenly seemed like nothing other than the rhythm of the Earth Mother herself, breathing under her feet and inspiring the dance.

"*Allah,* it's impossible!"

"What is it?"

"Go around again, Ramiz! Those—those troubadours! The one in the centre, dressed like King Shahriyar or someone—but it cannot be Haroun al Muntazir! What would he be doing there? Could he—" Yusuf licked his lips, which had suddenly gone dry. "Surely it is impossible that *he* is after us?"

"Ridiculous," Ramiz said calmly. "But we had better stop and investigate."

"Eureka! There it is! The circus! Slow down and go around the roundabout again."

"That girl dancing. What's that on her stomach?"

"My God, you're right! A butterfly tattoo! Has to be her!"

"What the— Look at that sultan! Isn't that him?"

"I don't believe it! We've been chasing him to save his life from Ghasib and the man's travelling around dressed up as a *sultan?* What's that ring he's wearing? Is that the Rose? Impossible!"

"They do say Haroun al Muntazir has a unique sense of humour."

Harry watched Mariel dance with more appreciation than he showed. She would win any sultan, heart and loins, as far as he was concerned. No belly dancer's costume had ever looked better. Mariel's high breasts, long waist and rounded hips were perfectly suited to the art.

Out of the corner of his eye he noticed something odd, something that shouldn't be there. With the hairs lifting suddenly on the back of his neck, he casually turned his head.

And met the gaze of Ramiz Bahrami.

A siren sounded in the distance, and the monkey dashed forward and muttered in his ear, "Cops coming! Head for the bus, pronto!"

The sultan's harem was breaking up with practised speed. In the middle of a fabulous backbend, her arms undulating above her, Mariel heard her music fade and disappear. "Let's go!" someone cried, and only then did she notice the sound of the siren.

Followed almost instantly by the shriek of brakes and crunching metal very close by.

A woman leapt out of a car which had been rear-ended by another driven by two business-suited Arabs. But instead of examining the damage to her vehicle, she came leaping over the grass, making a beeline for Mariel.

Meanwhile the circus crew were streaming past the woman in the other direction, heading for the bus. All around them the crowd, slow to react, was stirring in surprise. *"Mais qu'est-ce que se passe?"* *"Maman, pourquoi s'en va le cirque?"*

"This way!" she heard, and felt Harry's hand encircle her wrist and draw her in the direction opposite to the way the circus players were heading.

The two Arabs, Harry noted now, were close behind the running woman, one crying in Arabic that pierced the babble, "Look, he is actually wearing it! Isn't that the Rose?" All of them headed towards Mariel and himself.

The siren was louder now, and the police car was screaming down one of the four streets that met at the park. Meanwhile, traffic around the road that encircled it was at a standstill as people stopped to stare at so much mayhem.

Monkeys, harem girls and slaves fled pell-mell towards the eye-catching bus. Two smashed cars steamed in the middle of the roundabout. An Arab in a gold turban and billowing gold lamé trousers and a pretty, dark-haired harem girl in white and gold were tearing in the opposite direction, with several different people chasing after them. And a large bewildered crowd was milling around.

Harry led her flat out towards a small white Renault parked in crazy abandon up against the edge of the green, its doors open. "Get in!" he cried, letting go of her wrist and tearing around to the driver's door.

He had seen that the engine was running. Mariel had barely slammed the door when he had the car moving.

"Harry, whose car—" she began, but he interrupted her.

"Grab the bag on the back seat!" he ordered, and Mariel obediently turned to see a familiar red satchel. With a gasp, she reached for it and drew it into her lap. "Don't let it out of your hold!" Harry commanded.

He was weaving his way around the stalled traffic in the roundabout, heading towards one of the roads. Across from them the circus bus, too, was just starting to move. Harry turned down a road just as the police car arrived screaming into the roundabout, on the wrong side of the road. With a wild squealing of brakes it smashed into them. The police car skidded around till they were side by side.

The siren kept going. The *flics* were cursing and gesticulating and wrestling with their seat belts.

"Are you hurt?" Harry demanded, opening the door.

"I'm fine."

"We've got the Rose," he told her. "Let's get out of here."

She followed him out, passing him the satchel. Then he grabbed her arm and led her into pell-mell flight down the road leading out of the town. Behind them the police, extricating themselves from their smashed vehicle, called indignantly to them to stop.

They heard the sound of another crash. Harry, pausing to tear off the cumbersome curl-toed slippers and hurl them into a ditch, threw a look over his shoulder.

Traffic on the roundabout now was at a complete standstill, with cars turned in every direction and the sound of angry honking rising over the scene. The circus bus was stalled across two lanes, and monkeys and jugglers and harem dancers and male slaves were filing out of it. On the far side of the park, the two Arabs, a smartly dressed Frenchwoman, and Ramiz Bahrami and his cohort were spread out across the green, chasing after Harry and Mariel, like hounds picking up the scent. But in their way were dozens of astonished citizens, standing stock-still and gawping at the scene around them. Another siren sounded in the far distance.

The sound of their own wild laughter joined the cacophony as the sultan and his dancer raced down the road.

Twelve

"**O**h, my feet! Harry, I've got to stop! I can't go another step!"

The scenery was beautiful all around them—pine forests and rugged red earth and valleys with delicious streams—but hard on the feet. Mariel was walking on blisters, and some had burst.

Against all expectation, considering how they were dressed, they had managed to catch a couple of lifts, though not with anyone going very far. Anyone headed for Cannes or Nice was on the highway; the traffic on the back roads was local. They had explained to the curious drivers that they were on their way to the Fréjus Festival, which had caused a certain shaking of heads over the amazing peccadilloes of city youth.

Still, it had allowed them to evade pursuit. Once Harry had led her over a fence and along a track through a vineyard, where they had picked some grapes, mostly

unripe, and stowed them in the satchel. Later, resting
by a stream, they had washed and eaten some, and
grapes would form their evening meal.

Which Mariel needed now. They had caught more
than one glimpse of the Mediterranean during the afternoon, but they were on high ground, and it was still
miles away. She had hoped to last until they got to the
coast road, but now she had to admit defeat.

She was sure Harry was disappointed. He wanted to
get the Rose, whatever it was, to Cannes before anyone
caught up with them.

But in fact she had only preempted him. "Do you
see down there?" he said, pointing off the road to the
right to where a small barn was set under a tree. "I
have been thinking we should try to get inside. I would
prefer to be under cover tonight. Can you make it that
far, Mariel?"

It was a good choice. The place appeared to be a
horse farm, and the barn was set well away from the
main buildings and stables, at the far end of a paddock
near some sheltering trees that shielded their approach.

The door was unlocked. It was half filled with new
hay. There were a couple of saddles and other equipment, several horse blankets were flung over a railing,
and a battery-powered lantern hung from a hook.

"This is heaven!" Mariel cried. She grabbed a blanket and spread it out on the hay, carefully putting the
hairy side down. She pulled off her black wig and all
her jewellery and tossed it to one side. Then she flung
herself down and rolled over on her back, spreading her
arms. "What a day! I feel completely flattened!"

The setting sun was sending its last rays through the
open doors. The smell of new-mown hay on the country

air was intoxicating, and she heaved a sigh of genuine pleasure.

Harry set down the red satchel, straightened and grinned admiringly down at her. "You have an indomitable spirit," he said.

She blushed at the approval in his tone. He had lost his turban somewhere, and his face and chest were streaked with red dust and sweat. She had no doubt she looked the same. But the light in his eyes said she was an immensely desirable woman, and set her heart thudding.

"Our first concern is to find water."

Mariel lifted herself up on one elbow. "There should be a tap around. I saw a trough not too far away."

"Ah, yes?" Harry picked up a black plastic bucket and looked cautiously outside before they stepped out to make a circuit of the barn.

"There," Mariel said, pointing to a freestanding faucet a few yards away, and a moment later she was bent over, rinsing her face in the cooling gush and drinking from her cupped hands.

"You are sure this is safe to drink?" Haroun asked, for it was one thing he couldn't take for granted even after years of being in France—the abundance of good water.

"It probably is." Mariel grinned, wiping her face on the skirt of her costume as, with a muttered word, Harry bent to rinse his own head and drank deeply. "If it's not—well, I was going to die of thirst anyway."

He straightened with a smile. What a woman she was! Not once had he heard her complain about what was unavoidable.

"What was that you said before you drank?" she asked.

His smile broadened. "*'A'udu billah.* The prayer of those who are about to eat or drink something they are unsure of. It means 'I seek refuge in God.'"

"And does it make a difference?"

"Who knows? Disease starts first in the spirit, does it not? If I strengthen my spirit with conviction…"

She laughed, not in mockery. "Well, if I get sick and you don't, I'm converting!"

"I am sure Islam is not the only religion with such protective rites."

Mariel shook her head, realizing with a smile, "You're right. I'm sure *Grandmère* would have crossed herself before drinking that water."

Harry bent to fill the bucket, and they went back inside the barn. "Sit down and let me examine your feet," he said. Mariel sank down onto a saddle on the floor and Harry set the bucket in front of her, then moved over to where a couple of bottles sat on a beam under some tack.

"Here is some antiseptic," he said, returning with a bottle.

"*Horse* antiseptic?"

"Very dilute," he added quickly, suiting the action to the word by adding one or two drops to the bucket. Their joking enhanced the subtle intimacy of the little barn, and the familiar, hungry yearning stabbed her heart. She looked into Harry's eyes and saw an answering need, and the sweet realization swept her that here, tonight, it was inevitable that they would make love.

She smiled her acceptance, and watched his eyes close in lazy, approving acknowledgement.

And there was no urgency about something so perfect and predetermined. It would happen in its own time.

She unbuttoned the jewelled cuffs of her harem pants and rucked them up and put her feet into the cold, soothing water. She lifted them out again one by one as with strong sure hands Harry rubbed them clean and examined the soles for any sign of infection. Afterwards he rinsed his own feet, but refused her offer of a similar service, saying his feet were tough.

Then he stood to lift down the electric lantern, for dark shadows were by now creeping into the barn, and she felt a new kind of urgency emanate from him as he carefully closed the barn door and slid the bar across, then lifted the red satchel and placed it before him on the blanket in the lamplight.

"Now," he said. "Now we will see."

His face was grave. Mariel remembered what he had told her about the Rose—the lives and happiness of many people depend on it—and suddenly she believed it. What she saw in his eyes was not mere greed for some family heirloom. Whatever was in the satchel was of deeper importance than that.

He pulled the bag open to reveal bright blue plastic stretching over something. It was a supermarket shopping bag. Harry dragged it out, tossing the satchel aside, then pulled open the shopping bag to reveal cloth. That proved to be a T-shirt wrapping something.

It's like a Russian doll, Mariel wanted to say, but found she couldn't speak for the tension.

The T-shirt wrapped newspaper. The newspaper, unwrapped, revealed a small, round object wrapped in crumpled brown paper. Harry lifted it, held it in his hands for a breath, and at last unpeeled the brown paper.

He was holding a table ornament. One of those clear globes with an object or a scene inside, that swirls with snow when shaken.

It was swirling with snow now, but not so thickly that Mariel could not see the blood-red rose at its centre. So this was the Rose. She stared at it blankly as Harry held it up in the lamplight and gazed at it.

Well, it certainly wasn't for its monetary value that this trinket was prized. It was good enough of its kind, but Mariel was sure you could buy a thousand just like it for fifty or a hundred francs each.

"Is that it?" she asked in surprise. "Why is it so important, Harry?"

Harry started to laugh. The rose clasped in one hand, he fell back onto the horse blanket and gave vent to a deep belly laugh. "My God, we know that Ghasib hires fools, but this! How could any man be so stupid? Is this it, do you ask me, Mariel? No, this is not it! This is a rose, but it is a million miles from being *Warda al Jawadi*. Yet it is clear those two fools thought…"

His muscled brown stomach rippled with more laughter. "To think how many of us have been chasing all over the French countryside in pursuit of a cheap trinket that was probably being sold by the dozen in half the village market stalls we passed! It is too rich! And now they are all coming after us, believing that we have got the Rose!"

His laughter boomed up to the rafters, and Mariel was helplessly drawn in to laugh, too. "You take disappointment well," she murmured, when their laughter had subsided somewhat, setting him off again.

"What *is* the Rose, exactly?" she asked finally. "Won't you tell me?"

For answer he held up his hand, where the sultan's rings still glittered. "Do you see this ring?" He indicated a ring with a round pink stone, about an inch across. "The Rose is a ring, something like this, the rarest of pink diamonds, more than twice this size. Cabochon cut, nearly sixty-five carats. It is of inestimable value, both intrinsically and extrinsically. It has been in the al Jawadi family for generations, always passed by the ruling Sultan of Bagestan to his chosen successor, on the day he nominates him Crown Prince. To the people it was always a symbol of stability."

"But Bagestan doesn't have a sultan anymore," she prompted.

"No, not for over thirty years, since the coup that put this monster Ghasib in power. Nevertheless, before he died my grandfather, Sultan Hafzuddin al Jawadi, nominated my brother Ashraf to be Crown Prince, should we succeed in reestablishing the family on the throne. But he could not give Ash the Rose. It had been saved from the destruction only to be lost again. No one had known where it was since the death of Crown Prince Kamil, who died in the Kaljuk war.

"Suddenly it was found. Prince Kamil had entrusted it to his wife, but none of us knew of this, and she did not know the value of the Rose. She told us about it only recently. I went to the place where she kept it, but someone had been there before me—Ramiz Bahrami. *But someone already took the Rose.* I heard, and fool that I am, I did not demand a description of what it was they got! Let it be a lesson to me! Ash has always said I am too hasty. I see that he may be right."

"Then where is the Rose now?"

He laughed again and held up the crystal globe. "Since everyone is chasing this one, believing it to be the true Rose, the real one must be where it has been for the past five years—in London, masquerading as one of the ornaments on the coffee table of Rosalind Lewis. Now Rosalind al Makhtoum, my cousin's wife."

"Oh!" she cried. "But—that was in *Hello!* magazine! I saw pictures of their wedding when we were at your place."

"Yes," he said.

Mariel picked up the little ornament and examined the red rose. It had a drop of liquid like a tear on one petal. The snow had settled.

"Are you sure it isn't maybe concealed inside this thing?"

Harry shook his head. "Where? There is no room for it. No, this was not in any case how Rosalind described it to me." He frowned. "But who can Ramiz be working for? Those men who boarded the train at Lyon—I saw them again in the square back there, chasing after us. If Ghasib believes that I have the Rose, it makes sense that they chase me. But then on whose behalf had Ramiz stolen it, if not Ghasib's?"

He sat up and reached for the red satchel. The main compartment was empty, but there was a slim, zippered compartment on one side. Harry unzipped it, slipped his lean brown hand inside, and drew out a folded paper.

Inside was a sheaf of thousand-franc notes. On the paper was scrawled in Arabic, *Blessings on your enterprise.*

"A *belly dancer?*"

"Looks like they joined the circus, Hal. Every kid's dream."

"I can't keep up with her! And where are they now?"

"Who the hell knows? After creating more mayhem than you could believe, they disappeared down the road looking like some kind of crazy Gypsies."

"Are you going after them?"

"Sure." The voice went bright with sarcasm. "Just as soon as the X-rays are ready and my arm is in a cast, and when the garage has had time to fix the car, sure, I'll do that, Hal."

They sat drinking water and eating stolen grapes by lamplight, and it was a feast fit for the gods. When he chose and plucked one of the riper grapes for her, and slipped it between her lips, when she bit it between strong white teeth and the sharp sweetness burst onto her tongue, she almost swooned at the taste. When she held a grape between her lips and lifted her mouth for him, the kiss he left behind as he stole the little bulb was ambrosia to them both.

They both soon ate their fill, hungry for other things. Then Harry leaned up over her, and his eyes were dark with longing.

"But wait!" she cried, perhaps to prolong the sweetness a little longer, or perhaps because she was nervous of the intensity she saw in him. "I haven't danced for the sultan!"

He smiled quizzically at her. "The dance is meant to arouse the sultan. This is already accomplished."

Which only made her more nervous. Mariel rolled to her feet, then stood in the lamplight and began to press the earth with her feet, making her hips sway. "Make music for me," she commanded.

"Thus the harem girl to the sultan," Harry said wryly, lifting his hands. "I may have your head."

She smiled, showing her teeth. "No, you won't."

He began to clap his hands together, creating a beat, and her body responded to it as if his hands were stroking her, knowing that soon they would be. Her stomach undulated, her hips twitched beguilingly, her legs appeared and disappeared behind the delicate fabric. She turned her back on him and made the skirt of her costume shimmer with the movement of her hips.

He made the beat faster. Her arms danced like snakes climbing into the air as she bent backwards, her eyes throwing inviting glances, her hair tumbling down, and the hypnotic rhythm of her hips never ceasing.

She could hear music, the music of the Earth Mother's breath. She smiled at him with witchery in her eyes, and Harry reached out as she spun around, and captured her skirt.

Her breath caught in her throat as she stopped, looking down. He had her skirt firmly in one uncompromising fist, and she bit her lip at the strength and determination in that hold.

"Come," the sultan commanded, and the little dancer sighed and slipped down into his arms.

"All we know for sure is that they got away, Ash, leaving chaos behind. I've never seen a mess like that outside of a movie. Incidentally, Zounab al Safaak was among their number. There were also several others who had no business to be in that square."

Ash's breath hissed. "Where is al Safaak now?"

"Don't worry. He was a little too uppity with the French police—an Arab should never get uppity with the French police, Ash—and they searched his car. Apparently he does a little dealing on the side, or so they are willing to pretend. So we don't have to worry about him for a while."

Ash grunted. "Harry?"

"We're now looking for a sultan and a belly dancer, apparently."

* * *

His hand trailed beguilingly up her bare arm, and his fingers slipped under the little cap sleeves to press her shoulder. He looked into her green eyes and read in them a glow that he would never be able to resist. He bent his head and of its own accord his mouth found hers.

She had never been so hungry for the taste of a man, and as sensation exploded through her, she realized that she had been wanting him every second since she had seen that photo. Wanting him had been at the root of everything she had said and done.

Her lips parted and she invited his tongue to dance, thrilling with every hungry thrust that told her what dance he wanted to dance with her. Her hand stroked the powerful chest above her, slipped around under his sultan's robe to caress the delicious heat of him, ran down the muscled back to his waist, then up again to his strong male shoulder.

He was undoing the little hooks and eyes that held together the bolero over her breasts. Now he lifted his mouth from kissing and looked down as the two halves parted to reveal her firm breasts. The nipples were dark, small, and hungrily at attention, and obediently he lowered his head and kissed one and then the other, dragging his mouth over the tender, greedy skin so that she moaned.

His hands and his mouth stroked and caressed her with honey and heat, so that she melted into pure sweet sensation. Still she heard the rhythm of the dance, in his touch, his mouth, in her own mouth when she kissed his breast and his heartbeat was in her lips.

He drew her up to slip off the little bolero and toss it away, and then she felt his hands under her hips, drawing down the zipper and easing off the harem pants. A moment later his own gold and black trappings were in the hay.

The light went out, but she was already half blind with sensation. Through a high opening, moonlight streamed in on them, kissing his black curls, the powerful curve of his shoulder, her breast.

His hand drew aside the fabric of her briefs and she gasped with excitement as his fingers found her heat and his thumb toyed with the burning cluster of nerves that now lay exposed.

Her hips arched up to the touch, explaining to him better than words what she wanted, and he gave it to her, over and over, until that touch was no longer enough. Then, with a sudden impatience that thrilled her, he dragged off her briefs, threw off his own. Then he rose up over her, and his knee pushed her legs apart. His hand slipped under her buttocks to hold her body up for him, and with a loud groan, he pushed home.

Thirteen

———

A rooster woke them very early. They crept out in the half light, showered themselves with buckets of water at the tap, dried on the sultan's robe, then dressed and, carrying the satchel, set off down the road again.

Mariel had torn off the legs and skirt of her harem pants just above the knee and, by tying the lower half of the skirt across her front, created the impression—from a distance—of a skirt. There wasn't much they could do about Harry's gold trousers, but when he pulled on the T-shirt that had wrapped the rose, he looked like someone who might well be en route to the Fréjus Festival.

Or a Gypsy, perhaps. But they had money now. They could buy something as soon as the stores opened. They had packed up everything in the red satchel and set off to the sound of birdsong.

"So all those stories you were telling people were

the truth," Mariel said as they walked. Ahead and to
the left the sun was rising with breathtaking splendour.
Below, down the mountainside, was a thick spread of
pine forest. Beyond they could see the Med. The air
was fresh and cool, and she felt as though she were
watching the dawn not just of one day, but of the whole
world. As if the night just past meant everything was
new.

"I do not manage a rock band," Harry pointed out
mildly. "And I am only rarely called on in my capacity
as cat burglar."

"But everything else. But I don't understand—if to
protect your lives your family have all been living in
hiding since Ghasib took power, why were you telling
everyone the truth? Aren't you afraid that it will get
back to him? Especially if those men were sent by him,
as you suspect."

"But you saw the story in the newspaper," he reminded her. "This is part of a campaign to let the world
know about us. The time for secrecy is over. Very soon
now my brother will reveal himself, and demand that
Ghasib step down. Before this day, we hope to orches-
trate an awareness in the West. Because Ghasib trades
with the West, sells oil, buys arms, people are reluctant
to look at what his regime does. But they must be made
to see."

"And in Bagestan, too? Do you have to build up
support there?"

He shook his head. "There is all the support we could
wish in Bagestan, if we can only mobilize it, and convince the people that we can win. The man is a monster.
The people hate him. That station manager at Lyon, for
example. He was a Bagestani."

Mariel opened her mouth on a long breath of understanding. "Oh, was *that* it?"

"Did you notice that he limped? He is a refugee from one of Ghasib's infamous prisons, no doubt. He nearly wept when I told him, as you saw."

"Yes."

"The worst thing would be if the people became convinced that we might fail, and that, in the aftermath, the Islamic militants might take control. They will not rise against Ghasib if they fear that outcome."

"How great is the danger of that?"

"Almost none, if the people hold."

"Do you wish you had been your grandfather's choice? Would you like to be the new sultan?"

"I? I would hate both the responsibilities and the restrictions of such a role," Harry told her, and she couldn't help the smile that stretched her mouth. "Ashraf has been raised to know it is his duty. My cousin Najib and I joke that if anything happens to Ash we will have to toss a coin—and the loser will become sultan in his place."

"So what will you do after the restoration?"

"As Prince Omar's Cup Companion I have been largely engaged in foreign trade. When I resign my place with him, *insha'Allah,* I will manage trade negotiations for Bagestan. I hope to arrange to be based still in France."

It was a long, painful walk before they finally reached a town where the stores were opening. The first thing Haroun did was to change some money and make a phone call to Ash in London.

"Dammit, Haroun, is that you finally? Where are you?" Ashraf asked, in angry relief. "What is going on?"

"Never mind now," Harry said. "We'll be at Cannes later today if the traffic isn't impossible. Meanwhile, listen up. This is important. You remember I told you that someone had taken a certain article that belongs to you?"

"I remember," Ash said dryly.

"Well, they didn't. As far as I can guess, it's still where it was."

"What? It was never picked up?" Ash gasped.

"No. I'm almost sure, because I've got the thing that was picked up and it's not the right thing. Unless I've been the victim of a very elaborate decoy play, and I don't think I was."

The last few hours were the worst of the whole trip. The traffic along the coast road was at a standstill much of the time, and the taxi's air conditioning wasn't really operational. But it was the only taxi available.

They arrived at last, and then Harry leaned forward to direct the driver along the docks to the right berth. They passed hundreds of sailboats of various sizes, and motorboats and motor yachts, and then they came to the dock where the really huge yachts were moored, and drew up in front of the most beautiful and luxurious thing Mariel had ever seen floating. Her father had a small yacht, after all, and she had been aboard several large luxury yachts, but this kind of yacht was owned only by the world's richest.

All was in readiness for their arrival. The captain put out to sea as soon as Prince Haroun and his companion were aboard.

"What have you found out about Ramiz?" Harry asked Ash, who was still in London.

"Prince Karim says Ramiz went undercover on an assignment for him, while Karim let it be known Ramiz was missing. Karim and Ramiz were the only ones who knew. Everyone else was allowed to believe Ramiz might be dead.

"His assignment was to infiltrate the group trying to undermine the monarchy in Barakat. That group has apparently now decided they have an interest in preventing us from replacing Ghasib. It's something we should have foreseen—if they can foster a takeover by Islamic militants in Bagestan, they've got an important ally in their own efforts in the Barakat Emirates."

"*Allah,*" Harry breathed.

"It all makes sense as far as the Rose is concerned, doesn't it? Whoever is behind the Barakati unrest must have got the leak right in Rafi's palace, probably taping conversations when the Rose was being discussed, or when Rosalind phoned the woman in her apartment to tell her you'd be picking it up."

"So, you think this isn't a leak in our own organization at all? Can we be sure of that?"

"We're getting closer to it. What Karim and I are guessing is that Ramiz has worked his way into such a position of trust with the organization that he was one of the men sent to pick up the Rose. And he deliberately bungled it, either picking out the wrong rose, or not speaking up when the other man did. And then, apparently, he did his best to stall, to delay the moment when someone would recognize that it was the wrong rose."

"He must have recognized me on the train. Maybe even beforehand—in the Gare de Lyon. I wonder if he engineered that conversation right beside me, to let me know I should get on the train to Nice? Probably he thought he would find a way to talk to me during the trip," Harry added. "And when we were unexpectedly tossed off the train, he must have got off himself.... Looking back, it does seem a little too neat that the car was left running, and with the Rose in the back seat. Well, we owe Ramiz. And a few others, by the way. We'll have to have a little celebration for the people who helped Mariel and me in the palace when, *insha'Allah,* you're living there."

"Mariel is staying on board with you?"

"Yeah. She's another who'll be very happy when Ghasib's gone. Turns out he steals technological secrets from her American cousin."

Ash sighed. "I suppose this will all be unravelled in time."

"Well, yes and no. I'll be marrying her, Ash."

"Marrying her!"

"If we succeed, I mean. There may be nothing to offer if Ghasib gets the better of us, yes?"

"You've only known her a few days! Harry, you're too impet—"

"They were very trying, difficult days, Ash. You find out a lot about a woman in circumstances like that. She's a woman in a million, and I know she'll never say to me, *oh, Harry, you're so impetuous,* or *Harry, isn't that dangerous?* or *but won't you miss me if you're gone so long?*"

Ash had to laugh. "We did get the idea that she was as crazy as you are," he said dryly.

"Yeah. Crazy, and beautiful, and wild and free. So I won't be mentioning for a while that we're going to get married, Ash. I wouldn't want to spook her."

Ashraf understood the unspoken message behind his brother's light tone. Harry's personal happiness, too, now depended on their enterprise being successful. "Sure. Well, I'll do my best."

Harry didn't answer that. "When is the strike going to be settled?"

"Probably tomorrow. I've got to attend a charity function here in London tonight. If the strike's over, I'll see you late tomorrow or early the next day."

"I'll find some way to amuse myself till then," Harry agreed.

"He's who?" Hal Ward demanded incredulously.

"One of the grandsons of Sultan Hafzuddin al Jawadi," Mariel said.

"And who's he?"

"You'll be hearing a lot about him over the next little while. There was a coup in Bagestan, and he was ousted, back in 1969. That's when Ghasib came to power, Hal. The grandsons are going to restore the monarchy."

"Mariel..." Hal began warningly.

"That's the same Ghasib who's been getting Michel Verdun to steal your secrets, Hal."

"Where has your hair gone?" Harry murmured, coming up behind her as Mariel stood at the railing looking out at the lights of Cannes. They had cast off a few minutes ago and would be sailing down to St. Tropez while they dined.

He clasped the railing on each side of her, preventing her escape, as he had done once before.

"The hairdresser said the dye had ruined it, so I told him to cut it all off."

Harry laughed aloud. "With so little fuss?"

"I was due for a change."

"It is pleasant to have your neck so available," he said, bending to kiss it, and sending shivers of anticipation down her spine.

"I'm glad you like it."

"It is very chic," he said, striving to keep things light. "You look like a celebrity. Shall we invite *Hello!* magazine on board to take our pictures?"

She turned around in his hold and clasped her hands on the rail behind her. He had changed from the cream cotton sweater, navy pants and deck shoes that he was wearing earlier into an impeccable black dinner jacket, and he looked even more devilishly attractive and perfectly at home.

"Do you want to? Will it promote your cause?"

The yacht was beautiful, reminding her of one of those ships, always being reconstructed in the movies, that used to sail down to Aden in the nineteen thirties, filled with elegant white-linen-draped women and their smart snakeskin luggage.

And apparently she was going to be one of those women, at least for the duration. When the maid had opened the closet doors in Mariel's stateroom, she could only laugh at the sight of a rack of clothes purchased for her from the most exclusive designer boutiques in Juan-les-Pins and Cap Ferrat.

It was like being let loose in a toy shop. "If there is nothing there that you like, of course you will go shopping," Harry had explained. But there was nothing not to like, and she could hardly imagine that there was anything else to buy. Swimsuits, dresses, pants, shirts, gowns and the most exquisite pieces of lingerie obviously designed for evenings aboard *à deux*....

Tonight, he had told her, they would sail a little and dine and sleep aboard. Her heart hadn't stopped thumping with anticipation all afternoon. Now at last she had a chance to dress in the way she would like Harry to remember her when the magic was over.

With the help of the stewardess detailed to act as her personal maid, Mariel had chosen an emerald-green silk taffeta evening dress with a corset-like bodice that left one shoulder bare. It was spangled across the front with tiny diamanté that glittered under the lights as she moved. With the stewardess's help she had put matching sparkles in her short hair and, from the jewel case she was offered, had chosen a diamond tennis bracelet and diamond earrings. On her feet were soft green leather mules.

It was a far cry from Emma the working girl. Another facet of this fascinating woman, Harry reflected, as he drew her gently into his embrace and bent to brush his mouth over her always kissable lips.

"No," he said roughly, in answer to her question. "I don't want anyone to take pictures. I want to keep you to myself."

Fourteen

Later she took off the dress and the diamonds and slipped into silky peach-coloured pyjamas and robe, with lace over her breasts and inset into the shoulders. She washed off her makeup, sprayed on a touch more perfume, and then, her heart thudding with the day's accumulated anticipation, she went into the big, luxurious stateroom where the bed was softly lighted and invitingly turned down for them, and Harry was waiting.

He had changed, too, and was wearing navy pyjama bottoms and kimono. She went to him and slipped her arms around his bare waist under the robe, delighting in his warmth.

He threaded his hands through the spiky curls and looked down into her face. "You are so many women," he said. "And yet, you are always yourself. That is rare, in man or woman, to be so true to oneself."

"Is it?"

He gave her an impatient shake. "You know it."

Mariel laughed. "Kiss me, you fool."

He caught her head between his hands and gazed down into her eyes, his own sparkling with the devilment that stopped her breath in her throat. "Kiss you?" he whispered, as though her command had ignited some fire in him. "Yes, I will kiss you. And what else?"

He was so sexy, and his voice had taken on deeply erotic undertones, so that her blood was already rushing around her system like a trapped animal.

"What do you suggest?"

He laughed, and dragged her tight against him, pressing his mouth against hers. For an endless time it was enough, their lips damp and seeking, their tongues toying and tasting and promising. Her hands pressed his back, stroked his arms and his neck, her fingers tangled in his hair.

His kiss was honey, and sweetness melted out from the touch of his lips to every cell. "You're delicious," she murmured drunkenly, when he lifted his still hungry mouth. "I didn't know I could get drunk on honey, but I can."

He groaned, and kissed her again, dragging her robe down to her elbows, his fingers sliding under the sleeveless pyjama top to stroke and press her shoulders.

Every cell seemed to have its own electricity supply, firing and misfiring so that she cried out with every new touch. He dropped her silky negligee to the floor and pressed his lips where the lace of her top exposed her throat. He ran his hands down over her buttocks, then lifted her to fit her body against his.

They both moaned and pressed against each other, shocked by the hunger that consumed them. His hands slid under the silk, down over the skin of her rump, and dragged her closer while his hard flesh leapt against her through the fabric.

He lifted her to the bed and laid her down on it, while, with a desperation increased by what it fed on, his mouth savaged hers. Her legs lifted and clung around his hips. He lifted his head and, leaning his arms beside her head, thrust his sex against hers through the layers of silk. She cried out with hungry expectancy.

Mariel pulled at the neck of his kimono, and he lifted and tore it off before his hands caught her silky pyjama top and drew it upwards to reveal her breasts. He grunted at the sight, pulling the silk over her head and tossing it aside as his mouth came down and captured a nipple, and his tongue rasped against it, over and over.

She was melting. A core of electricity burned white-hot through her. She opened her eyes and looked into his face, and it was like seeing his picture for the first time—excitement leapt in her, and her heart reached out to him and her body yearned.

"Harry," she whispered. "Oh, Harry! Please!"

It struck him a blow that left him breathless. He could not resist the plea. He lifted her hips and pulled the bottoms off and down her legs, then dragged his own pyjamas off.

She cried out as he entered her, her head snapping back with the pleasure. He caught her hips in his hands to hold her there for him, and drove into her again. And again and again, and each time she cried out wildly.

Her cries put him over the top. He exploded in her and then was instantly hard again, so that he scarcely missed a beat in his rhythmic stroking.

"There has never been anything like this!" she cried once, hardly knowing where or who she was, only discovering that pleasure was a natural force, expressing itself irresistibly through body and soul, that was never satisfied. At each release her need moved up another notch, so that each one made her hungry for more.

For him it was the same. Each release only tantalized him with a promise of some ultimate explosion that would destroy and re-create him at the same time. A love that would consume him.

It was this they had been waiting for, this they had each seen, without knowing it, in the other. That together they would cross a frontier into a new existence where pleasure and love were the same. They clung, and pushed, and turned, and they pulled at themselves and each other, groping for that ultimate joy that urged them on and on.

There seemed no shape, no posture, that they could not achieve. She knelt while he stood behind and hammered into her until she collapsed with pleasure; he lay flat while she rose over him, thudding down and down until he clung to her hips and held her while his hips bucked.

At last it happened that she lay with her back against his chest, her arms and body spread helplessly, exhausted. He was on his back under her, driving up into her body.

His hand found her centre, and as he stroked her with tiny movements, a new, burning pleasure began to uncoil in her. She held her breath as if to listen, and his hand went remorselessly on, stroking and teasing that cluster of overheated nerves that seemed to be a knot of light filaments reaching out to the ends of being. Drawing love both from and to her being.

Pleasure burned up inside her, and she lifted her arms

over her head to stroke his hair, wishing she could kiss the pleasure back into his own mouth.

"Harry!" she cried, as the spiral grew and expanded, and now he could feel his own pleasure beckon, as her body clenched spasmodically around his, again and again, drawing it from him. He drove hard up into her, once, twice, and the pleasure wrapped her heart, opening it onto a world of limitless love. It flooded out then, and swept her, with a power that made the light go black.

Her whole being arched and writhed. She wailed as it rushed over her, and the cry summoned up the same flood of overwhelming longing and love in him, so that he need do nothing but give himself up to it.

It swept them, shook them, so that they helplessly cried each other's names. And they soared to a place called Perfection and, reaching it, as humans must, fell back again.

She turned in his embrace then, and he pressed a kiss against her breast, tasting her heartbeat with his life.

"I would like to show you Barakat one day," he said in the morning, as they stood waiting for their breakfast with nothing around them but blue water. A soft delicious breeze caressed them, reminding them each of how love had touched them in the night.

"Barakat, not Bagestan?"

"I was born and raised in Barakat. I do not yet know Bagestan. My father was Prince Wafiq. He was forced to flee during the coup, and I have been there only once or twice. But naturally I would like to show you Bagestan, too, if you wish it."

Mariel smiled and turned as he led her to the table. "On the *Dhikra?*"

"Or perhaps on *Ma Fouze,* my own sailing yacht. Do you sail?"

"Oh, yes. My father taught me when I was a kid and I've always loved it." This yacht was magnificent, but Mariel liked to feel the sea spray in her hair.

"Mariel, I have something to say to you." He lifted his head as the steward appeared with a platter of delicious-looking cut fruit, and wondered how long it would be before he could tell her the true depth of what he felt.

She caught her breath but could say nothing. After a moment he went on.

"My brother suggests, and I agree with him for once, that you and I may still be at risk from those who were chasing us. He would like us to stay out to sea for the next two or three weeks."

Her heart kicked. Two or three weeks? Did he intend to dictate now exactly when they would go their separate ways?

Well, she might have something to say about that.

"In a day or two Ashraf will arrive, and the yacht will be the centre for meetings and discussions with many different people as our plans develop. We can stay here on the *Dhikra,* or…"

One day at a time. That was what her father had advised her to do when she was distraught over the breakup of her parents' marriage. *Mariel, don't live it all now. Take one day at a time.*

But sometimes that just wasn't possible.

"Or we can sail away by ourselves?" she suggested, as the steward helped her to some of the tropical fruit. She smelled the odour of fresh lime and thought that it was a scent that would forever bring this moment back to her. When her future seemed to hold its breath.

"Not very far away. I will have to come aboard for meetings. But the *Ma Fouze* is small enough to be handled by two. We would be alone except when we chose not to be."

"For two or three weeks," she repeated levelly.

"If we succeed, the danger will be past in a very few weeks."

She tilted her head at him. "And then we part."

He did not answer.

"It might not be as easy as that," she said slowly.

He looked at her, and there was an expression in his eyes she hadn't seen there before. Her heart beat painfully. She took a deep breath, wrapping her courage in her two hands.

"I can't guarantee to go quietly in a few weeks."

His jaw clenched. "If we fail, Mariel, nothing is certain."

"One thing is certain, win or lose," she said. Her voice cracked with fear and feeling.

He was motionless. "What?"

"I love you, Harry." She saw fire leap up behind his eyes. "I can't agree to sail away with you for three weeks if it means that when it's over I just take a walk. If I go with you now, you have to understand that it's because I love you and I think I'll love you forever."

"Mariel, I cannot hear this now. If we fail—"

She almost laughed. "Do you know what? I fell in love with you when all I had was a photograph. And I was still in love with you when I thought you were a cat burglar. And then you started telling all those ridiculous stories and all I could think was that I had given my heart irrevocably to an accomplished con man. So you can't expect me to stop loving you if I learn that you aren't, after all, going to be the brother of a sultan."

He was on his feet, drawing her up into his embrace. She slipped her arms up around his neck and looked into his eyes.

"I love you, Mariel," he said, and her heart leapt into fluttering flight, leaving her breathless. "I have never felt for a woman what I feel for you—love, and passion, and admiration for your heroine spirit. I would not have told you, not till we knew the end of our efforts. It is your own courage that makes me confess.

"But you must understand how it is. If we fail, in a few weeks anything may happen. I may be dead, or worse—in one of Ghasib's prisons."

"We'd better think about escape plans, then," she suggested. "I wonder if the Travelling Circus could be of help there?"

He laughed and thought that, even loving her as he did, he had nevertheless underestimated her. "And if the Travelling Circus was not successful?"

"Do you think Monsieur Saint Julien has any experience of wartime escape from the Germans that would be useful?"

He shook her arm. "Mariel, be serious."

"All right, let me think." She put her finger to her chin. "Hmmm, in that case, I guess I'd have no choice but to hang around waiting for you."

He looked at her, a smile in his eyes that melted her where she stood, and she saw that he accepted it.

"And what shall we do with the next few weeks, my brave heroine?"

"Well," she said, "as it might be our last few weeks of freedom, then let's be free."

Sailing with Harry on the wind. She knew the thought pleased him as much as it did her.

Epilogue

"We're starting to understand the chain of events," Ash said. "Ramiz thinks Ghasib has put a mole inside the organization that is working to undermine the monarchy in Barakat. That mole passed on information about the discovery of the Rose to Ghasib via Verdun, but too late for Ghasib to get hold of it himself."

"It must also have been through that mole that the photo of me was sent to Verdun," Harry suggested.

"Yes. It seems a third man was sent along with Ramiz and his partner when they picked up the Rose, and that man was instructed to photograph anyone else who went to that apartment that day. Of course they hoped to get some line on us, but I don't suppose they expected what they actually got."

"Have you seen it, Ash?"

No need to explain what he meant. "Yes, I've seen it."

"And?"

"Harry, it's indescribable. That stone has got a glow inside it men would kill for. You've heard that, I've heard it, but it is beyond expectation. There is nothing like it."

Harry glanced at the coffee table, where newspapers in several languages were strewn, all of them more or less chewing over Ghasib and the Bagestani people's search for their sultan. It was a sign that the public relations campaign was under way.

"So it's begun?"

"It's begun," agreed Crown Prince designate Ashraf al Jawadi. "There's no turning back. It's win or lose now."

*   *   *   *   *

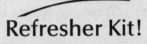